Where the Heart is

Ruth Adams

ISBN: 9798 8591 3533 2

Prologue

St Anthony watched over the street. If he could speak, oh the stories he could tell; of a teenage sister trying to be a mother to her young brothers, of a man down on his luck who had sat on the pavement with nowhere to go, a beautiful woman who had turned her back on her family to set up a life that had become increasingly fraught with violence and fear. What had become of all these lost things? Had the saint kept and found them, or did they have a way to go yet?

A few years have passed

Liz could hear the bricks being torn down if she opened her window. Her little bungalow didn't have a direct view of the church, but she preferred it that way. Out of sight but, as her sleepless nights would testify, never far from her thoughts. Two years ago, she had had to concede that the congregation was never going to keep the church running. There had been a flurry of business but that had dwindled. The last service had been John's funeral. A fitting end. Since then, Julie and Simon had been inseparable she heard. The age difference didn't seem to matter to either and they both had a glow about them that Liz was pleased to see. Christine and her mum had been there too, but the meeting between her and Tony never transpired. He was there, not sitting on the ground in tattered clothes with a dog Faithful on his lap, but standing proudly in a sharp suit with an unrecognisable combed and washed four-legged friend on a lead beside him. His eyes were searching for someone but he left without finding her.

After that day, Liz had admitted that there was nothing more that she could do, and no-one else had stepped up. All at once, she only saw the crumbling, empty pews and heard the tinny duet of her stalwart congregation. It broke her heart, but there would be new beginnings somewhere else. She had to believe that.

They had given her a lopsided cake and florally card and that was it. She used the retirement fund to put a deposit on her little house and moved out two months later. Since then, she had believed the cheerful lie that it was a new chapter. She still bent her protesting knees and prayed for all the people on her mind, but saw very few of them now. Some days she drove down to the church and looked up at her St Anthony. Even as the walls started to be demolished around him, he stood strong. But her heart asked, for how long?

She knew that the remnants of the congregation were going to the glossy St John's with the flashy white-toothed vicar there. She couldn't stomach it and had her own Sabbath rest watching the BBC services on a Sunday by herself instead. She knew it wasn't ideal, but felt that there was something waiting for her to do in time, if she kept her eyes open for it.

There was one person who kept coming back to her thoughts. She hadn't seen him for at least twenty years. She wondered if he was still about, and what he was doing now?

A new home

Jimmy took one last drag of his cigarette, threw it on the tarmac with the others and put a bit of chewing gum in his mouth. He gestured to the tarpaulin-cloaked statue,

"Where's this going to now?"

The other builder shrugged,

"Dump I expect."

Jimmy walked over to the trailer and lifted the cloth off,

"I used to look up at this fellow every morning on my way to school, willing him to cancel classes and magic away the teachers. Never worked."

Andy, his workmate, laughed,

"And still you asked him. Sounds like a pointless prayer to me. To a bleedin' bit of rock."

A white van arrived and two men in green council uniforms bounced out. They nodded to the other two and made their way over to the statue.

"Where's it headed?"

"Landfill."

"That's a shame."

The council worker shrugged,

"You got a better idea?"

Jimmy thought. He looked up at the place where the saint had stood for decades and felt a strange fuzzy feeling come over him. He walked over and touched the statue,

"Can you leave him with me until I make a few phone calls?"

The men shrugged and turned to light up for another smoke.

Five minutes later Jimmy was still staring at his phone with no notion what to do. He knew that woman vicar was long gone. And the social worker he'd met way back had also moved on. He looked down at the statue and then across at his car. It would never fit. He scratched his crew cut head and made his way over to the two men,

"Any chance you could take him to my house? I can't get hold of anyone right now. It's two minutes away."

One of the men slapped his thigh and roared with laughter.

"What you gonna do? Sit him in your lounge and make him tea?!"

Jimmy flushed,

"Better than being in the dump."

The other one shrugged,

"It's all the same to me. Give me your address and we'll drop him off for you."

Jimmy tried not to think about the craziness of what he had done. The men loaded their van and drove off with the saint before he could change his mind. He closed his eyes and hoped for the best. Sure how bad could it be?

His workmate was shaking his head,

"Man, you are something! Always feeling sorry for people passing by and wishing you could do something. But a ruddy great statue? That's taking the biscuit!"

They both turned back to sorting the rubble. Any bricks that were still intact could be kept for re-use. The rest was picked up to be reduced into concrete. As Jimmy threw the broken stones into the skip he knew that he had done the right thing. The next step would become clear soon enough. He had been stuck many times before and it had always worked out, one way or the other.

The day passed quickly enough and then Jimmy was sitting in his beat-up green Peugeot outside his house. The night was already creeping steadily into the day, and darkness was starting its fight against the remaining light. He got out and looked to the empty windows. For all the people he had helped over the years, there was no-one to welcome him home. The front door clicked behind him and his steps echoed back as he walked to the garden.They had balanced the statue between two unkempt bushes. Jimmy cursed under his breath; it was a lot bigger than he'd thought and in the dusk, a bit creepy. Plonked there in his small garden, it looked ridiculous and out of place. There were only a few broken off branches, and they had placed them on the saint's outstretched arms. Or had he done that himself? He certainly seemed pleased with himself. Jimmy hit his forehead. Get a grip man. He looked at the long grass and the flower beds filled with moss and dandelions. He remembered how neat mum had kept them, changing the bedding plants with the seasons and raking away any unwelcome leaves or weeds. His heart sank,

"If you do have some sort of power then could you use it to tidy the garden for me?"

Jimmy laughed a little then looked over the hedge to make sure no-one had heard him talking to himself like a madman. What had he been thinking? His postage stamp of a garden was not the right place for a saint. But then, neither was the dump. Something in the back of his mind told him that there was a good reason for what he had done, he just couldn't see it yet. Most passers-by wouldn't even notice. The neighbours didn't have a clear view of his garden, unless they opened their window and leant out. And why would they? What would anyone have to say? He had only nodded at a few of them getting out of their cars. That was the sum of his interaction with anyone who lived on his street. The days of people unexpectedly popping into the house died when she did.

Hold fast Jimmy. It will become clear in time. He shook his head, made his way back into the kitchen, flicked on the fluorescent light and peered into the saucepan of stew he used for his dinner five days of the week. He ladled a portion out, clattered it into the microwave and then carried it steaming to his permanently set table. Tonight, for the first time in a long time, he put his dusty hands together, bowed his head and said a silent grace.

St Anthony saw it all.

The first morning

Jimmy had not slept at all well. His dreams were filled with people from the dark time in his past, that he would rather forget. He had lived alone since his mum had died nine years ago. He had never known his father, and mum had never spoken of him. She always did her best for him, working all the hours she could to pay the bills. Every Sunday, without fail, she put on her only twin set and walked out to St.Anthony's for church. When he was younger, she had taken Jimmy along. All he could remember was his stiff collar and tight shoes. They always sat in the same seats and in the window beside them there was a statue he never forgot. It was of two figures, one kneeling, the other holding him. No-one had ever told him about it, but he had made his own story up. It had to be someone helping the other person up. He wondered if he would ever be like them.

After every service at least four people would stand round mum and thank her. He recognised them all as they had been in their house one time or another. Usually in a state about something. His mother was forever making cups of tea and taking scones out of the oven. He had never thought when he was younger that they didn't have much either. It was only when he started to work himself he realised how hard it must have been to keep him fed and buy the ingredients for all those scones. She had never complained. Which made her rapid decline so much more of a shock. He looked down and blinked back the tears. Looking out at the statue, he knew that bringing it here, and every kind act he had ever done, were all because of her.

He looked up at the singing blackbird perched on the saint's shoulder. It was Saturday, and he had no plans. As usual. The kettle whistled, drowning out the blackbird. As he made his tea and waited for it to brew, he walked out to look at the statue. Then he shook his head and went out into his garden. He cleared all the branches that had been disturbed and used his hands to lift weeds and leaves from around the statue's feet. Sitting back on his heels, he tutted,

'As if it bothers you.'

The few flower beds needed sprucing up. Maybe he would go down to that big shop and get some bedding plants. Make it look nice. He chuckled to himself, it's not as if anyone else was ever there. Once mum died, the steady group of four visitors stopped and no-one ever thought to call. Oh well, he shrugged and went back in to pour his tea.

Later that day Jimmy found himself loading up a trolley in the place he hadn't been for at least four years. The last time was to get some pellets to get rid of the slugs that were wrecking his lettuce. After that year, he just bought salad in the shop. It was too disheartening to fight with creatures that couldn't help wanting to eat things that were right in front of them. The shop was improved since he'd last been there. The cafe was more open and there was a sign at the front, encouraging people to give money to the homeless. As he dropped a few coins into the bucket a well-dressed man appeared at his shoulder,

"Thank-you sir. I hope you're having a successful shop?"

Jimmy wished he hadn't put that ridiculous stone dog in beside his plants. He had thought it would go very well at the feet of his saint. To keep him company.

"I see you like dogs?"

Jimmy grunted.

"Stone ones are definitely easier than real ones. Take that from someone who has the real type." He laughed and walked away. His badge said he was the manager. Tony. Jimmy took his trolley to the till and paid. He nearly left the dog behind, but something made him buy it.

When he saw the paw prints beside St Anthony the next morning he thought he was going mad. Later on when he was planting his new pansies, he saw the culprit. It was mostly brown with floppy ears. When it came to the statue it lay down. But as soon as someone called 'Faithful!' its ears pricked up and it ran off. Jimmy stood up to watch it bombing down the road to someone who looked very like the man he had spoken to yesterday. Jimmy glanced up at the statue,

"Do you believe in coincidences?" He laughed, "Of course

you don't. You make them!"

Jimmy surveyed his colourful, neat beds and was glad they were ready for any dogs or people that might pass by. Because he had a happy feeling there would be more now.

Matt's family

Jamie glanced at Matt's rigid back and turned over the pages in his book. Matt tutted and muttered under his breath about peace and quiet. At that moment the front door slammed.

"What now?!"

Matt stood up and marched out of their room. There was a one-sided exchange with Simon in the hall which ended with one person leaving and the other walking sighing into the kitchen. Jamie went in after him,

"Hey Simon. How's things?"

Simon pulled at his tie, considering his answer,

"All good, Jamie. You?"

Jamie sighed,

"I'm sorry about him," he jerked his head towards the door.

"It's not your fault. He's just figuring out the lay of the land."

"How long do you think that'll take? It's been close to a year now, since - "

"Julie and I got together."

Jamie shrugged and smoothed down his hair the way that Simon knows Julie hates but wouldn't dare say so himself. He needed people on his side right now.

"So what did you make of the whole statue drama the other day?"

"I dunno. It's a shame."

The conversation dried up,

"And the golf? Did you enjoy it?"

Simon cursed himself. Too eager.

"Oh yeah, thanks for taking us. It's a fair sight off nicking golf balls to get a few quid."

Simon laughed too loud and cleared his throat.

Jamie bent to look in the cupboard for something else to say but shut it again with a thoughtful look on his face. Simon raised his eyebrows and waited. Nothing. The front door jangled open and they both watched Julie arrive, their relief palpable. She rushed over to Simon, the pair of them grinning from ear to ear. Jamie edged out of the room.

"Jamie! How's your day been?"

"Fine. Nothing new."

"Where's Matt?"

Jamie raised both hands,

"No idea."

"The story of our lives these days."

They all stood and looked at their feet.

"I'm going to ask him. These times out at night are worrying for all of us."

Jamie shook his head,

"I would just leave him be. He never smells of drink when he comes home."

Julie sighed,

"But he needs to say. Do you think he's seeing someone he is worried we won't approve of? A boyfriend? Because I'm fine with that."

"He's not gay Julie. But I don't think that has anything to do with it."

Julie narrowed her eyes at Jamie,

"Do you know something you're not telling me?"

"Don't be upset but I think he's trying to figure out who our dad was, and where he is now."

Simon sat down on the sofa all of a sudden and started to look at his hands.

"Sorry to tell you both, but he's not going to stop looking until he finds him."

"And what about you? Do you not want to go with him?"

"No. I made my peace with it years ago, after I took that sculpture thing, remember?"

"Is that why you don't go to mum's for dinner too?"

Jamie glanced from one to the other,

"I don't feel I need to. I'm happy here."

Julie teared up and then laughed,

"That's fine with me. We love having you here, don't we Simon?"

Simon cleared his throat,

"Of course."

When the three of them were at sitting down to dinner the door opened again. Julie groaned, "that'd be mother then."

"It's me!"

A grinning Lisa appeared. Jamie looked up and gave her a forced smile.

"I've got news!"

"Dear God, you're not pregnant again?!"

Lisa laughed and then caught Julie's tone.

"No! I'm past that now. I've rented the flat next door."

"With what?"

"I got a job."

"How?"

Lisa laughed again,

"An old pal hooked me up."

Julie sighed and put her hands to her face. Simon stepped in,

"Well, tell us about it. Where is it and what do you need to do?"

"It's in the canteen of the department store where you are too, Julie?"

Julie stood up and slapped her hands on the table,

"Was it Tony? Of course it was. You don't have many 'pals' do you."

Lisa stepped back, shook her head and whispered,

"I thought you'd be pleased I was taking responsibility."

Julie narrowed her eyes at her mum.

"I'll let that belated statement go. You're eighteen years too late Lisa."

Lisa nodded at Jamie, lifted her hand and turned to go. The door shut very quietly behind her.

"Well done, Julie. She came in all pleased and you just stamped all over it."

Jamie stormed out and two doors rattled in their frames behind him.

Julie dropped to the chair and started to cry. Simon pulled her into his chest. He knew there were no words to sort out this tangled, back-to-front situation. What child can be a mother to her own?

Eventually he spoke up,

"Don't be worrying too much Julie. These things have a way of evening out."

"I wish it was as easy as that. Years of experience have

taught me different."

Simon held onto her arms and leant back,

"And look at the amazing, strong, independent woman standing in front of me in spite of all that!"

Julie blushed and dried her eyes,

"Thanks."

They both moved into the living room and sat down, the sound of lashing rain hitting the gutters, wheely bins and discarded tins outside. Julie wondered briefly if her mum made it back to wherever she was currently living. After that Christmas when she waltzed into their lives as if nothing had changed, Julie had gritted her teeth and bitten her tongue countless times as Lisa came and went whenever she pleased. Sometimes she had slept on their sagging sofa, sometimes she disappeared for weeks. Julie tried to keep her expectations as low as they had been before, and flicked her responses off after the initial return. Better not to hope than be continually disappointed. The hardest thing of all was when she tried to be a mother. Once she had asked to go along to the teacher interviews at school but then forgot and it was left to Julie as usual. Matt had left after his GCSEs and was at college training to be an electrician. Jamie had chosen A levels in the subjects he liked, with no idea as to what he wanted to do beyond that.   She just hoped nothing, no-one, would knock them off course.

Matt passes by

Matt nodded his thanks for the £1 meal Lisa heated for him and left her ramshackle flat, taking a random turn away from his official home. He never really had a concrete plan of where he was going every night, he just knew he wasn't ready to face his big sister and her smug boyfriend. Well, Simon was all right, when he didn't try to act like he was his dad. Taking them for golf or telling him off for being late was not going to change the fact that he wasn't and never would be their dad. She didn't know yet, but Matt choosing to visit Lisa every day for tea was mainly because he wanted to find out who his dad was. He knew she knew. He'd play the long game if he had to. Jamie didn't care as much, ever since he had put the prodigal son statue back in the church, he had stopped looking. Matt, on the other hand, had increased his search. Some things, some people, just had to be found.

The dark was growing now. From about five, kids were walking home under street lamps, their faces lit up by rectangles of light from their phones. Matt took in the shabby uniforms of some, and wondered how they managed to pay for their cutting-edge technology. How many golf balls would he and his brother have had to sell if this was the done thing in their day? They had never managed anything more than a pack of fruit pastilles each. On a good day. Julie, to be fair, had done her best standing in for their absentee mum. There had been waves of money but they never knew when that would happen. Just like they never knew when they'd see their mum. The two things seemed to arrive at the same time. And never any sign of their dad, if he was still alive. Matt felt in his gut that he was. So he kept walking, looking for something that he thought was long overdue. After all this bad, surely he deserved something better? He brushed his wet eyes with the cuff of his duffel coat and carried on up the hill. He stared in at families eating toasted pancakes, siblings battling furiously on the xbox, a lonely boy watching Looney Tunes while his mum and dad shouted at each other in the kitchen behind him and then a man sitting at the feet of a familiar looking statue in his garden, drinking tea. He met Matt's searching eyes and waved. Matt raised his hand in response.

"You looking for someone, son?"

Matt stepped closer,

"No not really. What's that big church statue doing in your flowers?"

Jimmy stood up and walked over, still holding his mug,

"You remember him? Used to be on the roof of St Anthony's. Know it?"

Matt nudged the gate open and carefully stepped in,

"So how's it here?"

"They were going to dump him. I told them I'd keep him. Crazy old fool that I am." Jimmy shrugged his shoulders in his fading woollen jumper and chuckled.

"So what's going to happen to it now? I mean, no offence but it's pretty out of place here."

They both contemplated the statue.

"You know he's the patron saint of lost things? You looking for anything?"

Matt put his head down and tutted,

"I've walked past this guy my whole life and I've never found anything. Not a penny. Definitely not my loser of a father."

Jimmy took in Matt's glittering eyes and tightened his lips.

"Well, no amount of magic ever brought my dad within spitting distance either."

Matt dropped down on the damp grass and they sat in silence. Jimmy nodded over to his house,

"I did have a brilliant mum, but she's dead now so it's just me and this concrete lump here. You know, in her whole life, she never said who my father was. When I was young I used to make up stories like he was a spy, or he died fighting overseas, or something. It took a long time before I accepted that he was still alive but he didn't want anything to do with me. Or maybe he never knew I existed. I'll never know. Best to move on from all that guessing and wondering. It doesn't lead to anything good. You know?"

His question hovered unanswered. After a tense moment, Matt stood up and brushed his jeans down,

"I need to get going. I'll see you."

Jimmy stretched out his hand,

"It was good to talk. I'm Jimmy. I didn't catch your name?"

"Matt."

They shook hands and the younger loped down the path again, his hands deep in his pockets. Jimmy watched him go, and knew that his speech about giving up searching had fallen on deaf ears. This one was not ready to accept what he already has. Jimmy went back inside and looked around him. There were only faded photographs of mum on the mantelpiece. Nobody else. He held up his hand and counted on three fingers the people he had in his life now. They were not really in it though. Who would help him out if he got sick? Who would make him dinner if he couldn't do it himself? There had been a time of parties, too many people and too much drink. He had stumbled through in a haze of drunkenness until one day he had caught mum crying in the kitchen. Like she was breaking her heart. He had stood swaying in the door and knew she was crying because of him. That was the day he had stopped drinking, walked away from unhelpful 'friends' and re-built his life. That was the day, at the age of twenty-one, he grew up. He hadn't needed a father to show him the way. Just a mother.

Jimmy peered out in the darkness and was sure the saint had been smiling at him. Ridiculous. But maybe he should go back to the store and buy some outside lamps. Just in case someone came searching in the dark. He looked again at his fingers and touched one more. Matt.

Two other brothers

Tony looked up at the empty roof and down at the rubble. He glanced left and right, hoping for something, or someone, but sat down outside of the fence barrier instead. It felt strangely familiar and comfortable, until he turned round and remembered the saint he had always believed watched over him was gone. He stared down at the place he imagined the entrance had been and let himself think about a troubled, beautiful woman who looked to him, in all his hopeless state, to help her. He had not forgotten about her. All this time. He wondered whether she ever thought about him. His phone rang, breaking into his reverie. He started walking home as he answered.

"Tony? It's me."

Gavin had been calling him every week since he left more than four years ago. Slowly, one unremarkable conversation after another, they were building the sibling relationship they had never had before. Tony told him about the demolished church, the toppled statue. Gavin sighed,

"So they found someone else to drive that forward, after the shambles I'd left behind me. Have to say, I'm sorry that happened in the end. Maybe, if things had been different, I would have been able to stop them."

Tony raised his eyes heavenward.

"That's a stupid thing to say. All good with you?"

"The job is going well. People are starting to ask for my opinion again."

"And what about outside of work? Anything happening there?"

"Not really no. What about you? Any girlfriends?"

Tony flushed,

"Sure who would I meet around here?"

There was silence on the line then Gavin cleared his throat,

"I have met someone here."

"Really?!"

"Yeah, she cleans the office so keeps the same hours as hard-working me. And I think this is my chance to treat a woman right, after Christine."

Tony gripped his phone and tried to think of something to say,

"That's good you get another shot at it. Don't mess it up."

Gavin sighed and took his leave. Tony stared at his screen, pressing his lips together. He cursed, sat down on the seat behind him and let his arm drop. He sank his head into his hands and tried to slow down his racing thoughts. He didn't let himself think about the dream that had now grown wings in his heart, the hopes that were exploding in his mind. He had waited for such a long time, he couldn't quite believe he could start the process of showing Christine he was indisputably, unstoppably in love with her. His brother had stepped aside. He could only hope that the memory of him wouldn't mar how Christine saw Tony.

Faithful got out of her bed and walked over to rest her head on his knee. He put his hand on her head and started to stroke her velvet ears,

"What do you think I should do? Go to Christine and try my chances? Or just give up?"

Faithful's tail had started to wag as soon as she heard the name. She put her paws on Tony and barked.

"Ok ok. I'll go look for her soon."

Tony unhooked the lead, grabbed some poo bags and took Faithful out for her afternoon tear around. He never needed treats to lure her back. She lived up to her name, ever since he had given it to her, on the unsheltered street where they had both lived. As he walked to the park, with her trotting and sniffing by his side he looked down at the flowers lying broken by the path. There was no-one to gather them up now. He passed by the toilets without stopping, shaking away the horrible memories of scrapes of toothpaste and trying to get clean over a tiny sink with a smashed mirror. He had good memories too but he didn't know whether there was any point dwelling on them now. He looked up at the sky. It looked like it was going to rain. He'd best head back.

But where had Faithful gone? He caught sight of a flash of brown fur and ran after it, calling her name which still sounded ridiculous, especially when people were walking past him, a man by himself. He kept the dog lead visible so it was clear he had a dog and wasn't entirely deranged. Somehow, walking around shouting a word repeatedly was causing him more embarrassment than when he was homeless, sitting on a busy pavement. Then, he was more invisible than now, because everyone avoided looking at him. When Faithful's tail disappeared into a hedge he stopped calling as he looked up and everything became clear. He was there. Tony had a feeling that he wasn't the first person to find him either. He searched up and down the street. He even straightened his shirt and smoothed down his hair. When he rang the bell, his pulse started to race. He could smell her perfume. At least, he thought he could. There was no answer. No car in the drive either. He pushed open the gate and walked in,

"How did you get here? You saw her, didn't you? How did she look? Lost? Happy? Waiting for something? Waiting for someone?"

Tony looked at the unchanging face and knew it was a fruitless task. Praying might work but had he not been doing that ever since the last day he had seen her? And he wouldn't stop. If only she knew. Faithful was lying down close to the statue's feet, looking like she was there for a while. Tony sat down on the bench and thought. It didn't feel out of place to be sitting here in a stranger's garden. Probably something to do with the saint he knew so well. He had never thought that he was particularly lost. But maybe he had been. Maybe he still was. He knew everything he had before had been taken away, but he didn't miss any of it. He only missed *her*.

Tony stood, saluted the statue, whistled for the dog and set off. No point waiting and hoping for someone. When things or people were lost, they needed to be found. If they wanted to be that is.

Paw Prints

Jimmy went out early the next morning and looked at the story the muck was telling him. There were a couple of boot prints, a lighter few from what looked like a woman's pointed shoe and paw prints. He frowned over at the stone dog but knew in his rational head that a real one had been there. He sat down and tried to guess who had been in his garden when he was away. They had obviously all known the statue before and had found him because they were searching. Jimmy examined his hands. What about him? What had got into him and made him get the over-sized monument brought into his unremarkable garden? Was he searching too?

A brown dog jumped over his gate and sat at his feet, panting. The man from the department store came shortly after, his face red and apologetic.

"Faithful! I'm so sorry. It's a long story but I can't keep her away now she's found him again."

Jimmy watched Faithful sniff round the stone dog and nudge him to see if he was alive.

"That's ok. I have quickly learnt that putting a famous monument next to my house was bound to draw people here."

Tony sat down on the grass,

"Me and Faithful used to sit beneath this saint and his church every day. For hours."

Jimmy frowned and looked closer at the man sitting next to him. He had a faint memory of a heap of rags on the paving slabs outside but surely it hadn't been this man? Shame on him for never bending down and looking. He had been so wrapped up in his own struggles he hadn't seen anyone else.

"Were you there through the night?"

"Yes, for a few months. It was a bad time in my life. I had lost everything."

Tony brightened as he hauled Faithful onto his knee,

"But this one came along and saved me. There were other people too."

Jimmy bent his head and thought of his mum.

"Do you ever see them now?"

Tony's face fell,

"Sadly no. There is one I long to see again, but it's complicated."

"The woman whose footprints are over here?"

Tony stood up and squinted,

"Who knows. I thought that, I guessed, I hoped, she had been here but that was just wishful thinking."

"I wouldn't be so sure. Don't know how or why but this thing," he jerked his thumb towards the statue, "he seems to make unbelievable stuff happen. She'll be back again, I'd put my money on it.".

Jimmy watched as Tony stared at the ground, trying to push back whatever struggle he had been battling with. He put his hand on the once homeless man's shoulder and left it there for a moment,

"It can't be a coincidence that you're called Tony, or that you found yourself at his feet twice."

Tony gave a sad laugh,

"He's just a statue. I knew someone who would have said it's the God behind him who's the real deal."

Jimmy thought of his mother, and the church she so faithfully attended.

"Was it the vicar there? Liz somebody?"

"The very one. She's retired now. But I'm sure she's still working in her own way. You ever meet her?"

Jimmy stared into the far distance,

"My mum used to take me to her services, in St Anthony's. I never spoke to her though. You?"

Tony smiled,

"I was her first charity case. She dragged me off the street, into her church and fed me soup. That turned into a soup-kitchen for all and sundry. When the building was sold it stopped obviously. Shame."

"Were there many that came?"

"Couldn't tell you. That week was a blur of finding then losing my brother again. That was the last time I slept there."

"You have a brother? What happened there?"

Tony shrugged. Then he looked at his watch,

"We'd best get going so I'm in time for work, Faithful." The dog left her station beside the statue with reluctance.

"She can stay here with me if you like. It's a day off for me so I'm free."

Tony hesitated for a second but put Faithful's lead on and shook his head,

"Thanks but Faithful stays with me. I can't leave her."

Jimmy put his palms up,

"Fair enough. But if you ever think of it I'm here."

Tony started to walk away and just raised his hand when Jimmy called after him,

"If the owner of those footprints shows up again, I'll be sure to tell her you were here, looking."

Tony kept walking. But he didn't tell Jimmy not to.

Jimmy looked up to the statue,

"That's a cry for intervention right there. Did you hear it?"

A robin flew close by and started pecking at the bird seed Jimmy had scattered on the ground. When he scooped up a handful and offered it, the bird boldly perched on his hand to eat. They stayed like that for a few precious seconds before it flew away, leaving Jimmy looking after it and feeling for the first time in forever that he was of use.

The past comes back

The front door opened and slammed shut again. Simon took the final sip of his coffee and braced himself. Matt peered round the door,

"Oh, hi. Julie not back yet?"

"It's past eleven Matt. She's gone to bed. I'm just here to see you're safely in before I head back myself."

Matt's mouth tightened,

"You didn't need to do that. I'm fine without anyone fussing about it."

"Where were you?"

Matt started to walk away.

"It's a simple question."

He was at the door when Simon caught up with him and grabbed it.

"Let me out. This is not your house. You're not the boss of me."

"I know that. But your sister is worried for you. She needs to know you're not in trouble. Are you?"

"Of course not. I just want to do my own thing without having to tell the world about it."

Simon waited, hoping for more detail but it wasn't forthcoming. When Matt shut the bedroom door, there was some whispering between him and Jamie and then silence. Julie stuck her head out and raised her eyebrows, whispering,

"Did you find out where he was?"

Simon shook his head and raised his palms. She got beside him,

"Did you say anything else?"

"No. I think I'm the last person he would tell anyway."

"Do you think he is in trouble? How did he seem?"

"He's ok. If he says there isn't a problem, we need to take him at his word."

Julie sighed,

"I thought as they got older it would be easier. But it's a different kind of challenge now. Scarier."

Simon nodded, with nothing, no experience to offer. He stopped himself from thinking about where their real father was and whether he should look for him. If he had wanted to be involved, he had had years to step in but hadn't so…

"I'm glad you are around now. They had never had anyone like you before."

Julie smiled at him. He looked at her uncertainty and felt slightly terrified himself,

"Have you spoken to your mum about any of this?"

"What would be the use of that?"

The door bell chimed and Julie sighed,

"At this time of night?"

Lisa came in, speaking in a loud whisper,

"I saw your lights on. Is something up?"

Julie put her finger to her lips and walked in to the sitting room, beckoning Lisa to follow her. They both sat down opposite each other and Simon stood, his feet pointing towards the door.

"Is everything all right? Well, I saw Matt earlier so I know he's fine."

"When? When did you see him?"

Lisa looked from one to the other,

"He came to me for dinner. Did he not say?"

Simon looked over at Julie but elected to hold his tongue.

"Does he go over to you often?"

Lisa bristled,

"Most days actually."

"He never said. I've been worried sick about him, and now you're saying he's been next door with you?!"

"How is that a problem? I am his mother after all."

Julie's face was on fire with fury. Simon stepped in,

"We were both worried about him Lisa. He doesn't say where he is, you see. And comes back late."

Lisa shook her head,

"I always send him home before nine."

"Well he doesn't appear until eleven so how do you, as his 'mother', explain that?"

Julie kept her air quotes up after her question. Her face was red and she was visibly shaking. Lisa tried to hug her, but she stepped away.

"Well? Where is he going? You're the pro at disappearing.

You must know."

Lisa's head went down,

"He can't be going far."

"Has he said anything?"

"No. He did ask me about his dad but I don't know anything about that."

Julie's face cleared and she looked over at Simon,

"He's looking for our dad."

Lisa cleared her throat,

"His and Jamie's."

"Not mine?"

Lisa shook her head,

"Sorry love. I haven't seen yours since…."

Julie sat carefully down on the sofa behind her.

Lisa stood up and looked out the window,

"I haven't seen him again. When he didn't appear I just decided to carry on without him. I think I saw him again once but he just looked through me like he didn't remember me."

Julie stared at the carpet. Simon stared at her.

"What was his name?"

"I think it was Andy? Or Jonny?"

The daughter/sister/mother walked out of the room, leaving Lisa and Simon looking after her.

"She has had such a hard time of it you know, picking up the mess you leave behind. Much more than once."

Lisa paled, stuck her chin out and left the room. Simon did not call after her. He had no desire to take back his comments. Julie came back not long after her mum had left and sat beside him,

"I have never asked questions about him. I just accepted early on that he was never going to be in my life. But now? I know his name. Or sort of. And I know he never knew about me."

Julie started to cry a little and Simon held her tight. He knew that this was a tiny release of sorrow that she had carried and pushed down all her life. He found himself saying what he knew Liz would say,

"We all have a Father, no matter how dreadful the earthly ones were."

Julie looked at him with a frown,

"Do you believe that?"

"For the first time, I think I have to. There has got to be more to this hard life than what we have here. Liz is always saying that."

Julie shook her head,

"Well, she'd be pleased to hear you right now."

Julie patted him on the back,

"I'll get it one day, I hope." She stood up, "But now for bed. You can sleep on the couch if it's too late."

"No, I need to get back and find my suit for tomorrow."

They kissed, and he held onto her arms,

"You know I love you?"

She nodded,

"And I you. Thank-you Simon."

Lisa

Lisa took her time getting back to her new home. Her feet dragged on the concrete flags as she thought over Julie's anger at her. For not being the mother she should have been, for being unreliable, for being everything she shouldn't have been, and nothing Julie, Matt or Jamie needed. A young mother was pushing a screaming baby in a Silvercross pram in front of her in the near darkness. She was stopping every now and then to check her phone and take a swig of something, either irn bru or an alcopop. Her phone rang and she stopped to answer it. As she casually walked away chatting Lisa saw she had forgotten to put the brakes on. The pram started to roll. The baby kept screaming. Her mother kept talking to her pal. Lisa picked up her speed and grabbed the pram handle just before it bumped onto the road. Only then did the mum look over and realise she had forgotten the brakes and the baby. Lisa peered into the pram and made an tempt to soothe the baby. The girl swore at her and snatched at the handle,

"You leave my bairn alone!"

She spoke into her phone,

"Gotta go. Some hobo is trying to kidnap Dyslexia."

She tugged at the pram and Lisa held on.

"What are you playing at? Get your dirty hands off my baby!"

Lisa shrugged,

"She needs a pacifier. Or lifted. What did you call her again?"

"Dyslexia. It's foreign. Haven't come across anyone with that name. Have you?"

Lisa knew now was not the time to explain what the name actually was. Someone would tell her soon, surely?

"How old is she?"

"Seven weeks. So still at the screaming stage. I put a drop of this" she lifted up the alcopop, "in her milk but it didn't calm her down."

She shook the pram,

"Would you ever shut up?! I mean, for feck's sake!"

She lifted her drink to take her leave and walked in the opposite direction.

Lisa looked after her and her heart sank. She only had a handful of memories of her babies. The clearest ones were of her walking away. She didn't even know if any of them had cried more than the others. Or what their favourite toy had been. Or their first word. She had been there for Julie for longer than the boys. But her mum had done the lion's share while she went out with her 'pals'. She had only been seventeen when she had Julie so was too young to take responsibility. Lisa sighed. What a mess she had made of her life, and the lives of her children. If there were any successes, it was all down to Julie. She closed her eyes as she recalled her daughter's words, 'you are eighteen years too late'.

She shook her head and quickened her pace, turning back to her flat. Reaching in her pocket for her keys, she did a double take. Where were they? She looked up at Julie's blank windows. No-one was looking out, thankfully. She walked back, searching the path for her keys. No sign.

"Looking for these?"

It was Jamie.

"Oh thank God. Where were they?"

"Just on the step. I recognised the key ring."

Lisa took them from him,

"Thanks. Can you do me a favour? Don't tell your sister."

Jamie smiled and tapped his nose as he ran up the steps to his house.

Lisa gripped the keys tight and cursed her carelessness. How on earth would Julie ever respect her if she kept doing stupid things like that? She ran back and closed the door behind her, hoping no-one had seen. She flicked the naked lights on, dropped down on the hard sofa and let her breath slow. It was past midnight and she had an early start tomorrow. After that, she would do something useful, if his number was still the same. She checked her two alarms and climbed into bed. There was no room for another slip-up. She didn't want to hear those words ever again, *you're eighteen years too late*. Surely she deserved a break from all that now?

The day at work passed ok. Lisa got all the orders right and there were no complaints from customers. She was still shadowing another woman so any mistakes she might make were quickly corrected. When that ended, the real test would begin. But so far so good.

She sat on her inadequate sofa and scrolled through her contacts. He had never given her any other number than his mobile. She dialled it anyway. Straight to voicemail. She hung up and slapped her cheeks before re-dialling,

"Hi it's Lisa. Remember me? Anyways, just wanted to check in. The boys are fine. Jamie is studying and Matt, well, he's doing his bit too. I was just phoning to give you their address. In case you ever want to write or something. It's '8, River Park, B42 7SW'. Matt still asks about you so maybe you could send him something."

Lisa hung up and stared at her phone. Well, that's that. She'd not say anything until he stepped up, if that was still his number. She hoped it was, for Matt's sake. She knew he kept visiting because he was desperate to find out about his father. She just hoped that he would still want to see her if he got the answers he was looking for. She hoped they saw her as their mother. It was time for that burden to be taken off Julie. Lisa was ready, however late it was, to try and do her best for her children. That was one father contacted. Who knows where the other one was. She had never told him because she had never seen him again. It was a long time ago now. Did it really matter? Julie had never asked so maybe she didn't mind. She had cried when her granny had died, but had never known her grandad. He hadn't been on the scene much either. All these missing fathers. It was a jigsaw that could never be completed. Could they cope with the pieces that were left? Because that might be all they ever had.

Jimmy

The January days were done. Jimmy wondered if anyone
existed that liked that dark, interminably long month. He
looked down at the clump of snowdrops to one side of his
builders' boot. He only noticed them now, after years of
mum always pointing them out. The first sign of spring
she used to say. He ran his eyes over the statue and the
tidy beds on either side of him. He lifted off the stray
leaves and twigs that had blown onto his outstretched
arms. He adjusted the spotlights and straightened the
wooden seat he'd moved from the side in case anyone
wanted to take a bit of time. He laughed at himself. Time
to do what? It wasn't a chapel, just his unremarkable
garden with an oversized statue in the middle of a mainly
ruined flower bed. The base of the sculpture stretched far
beyond the narrow strip of soil. It really was not the best
place for it at all. The one advantage was that it could be
seen from the road, so if anyone was looking they would
see him. Jimmy had never thought beyond the initial
rescue from landfill. Would they come back and move it
sometime? Unlikely. Someone must know someone who
had the capability of moving it. Jimmy didn't. He went
back inside the house and came out with paper and pen.
Seeing as the statue was here, he should record the people

who had come to see it. He wrote down two names with a question mark beside another. Tony was convinced, or maybe just blindly hopeful that Christine, his long-lost love had stood here as well. Jimmy chewed on the end of the biro. Would they come back? He was pretty sure that Tony would as Faithful had made it part of her route. Matt was less likely. The woman possible. Anyone else? Well, he would not make any enquiries about moving it. Miracles took time and these lonely days, he had plenty of it.

Someone coughed close by. Jimmy looked up to see a beautiful blond turning on her heel when she saw she was not alone.

"Don't leave on my account! Come on in."

The woman stopped turning away and flashed a smile at him. He walked over and held his rickety gate open for her.

"Have you seen him before?"

She blushed,

"I spotted him a couple of days ago, and couldn't quite believe my eyes. He was at the church before?"

Jimmy took his cap off and gestured to the seat,

"They were going to chuck him, and I couldn't let that happen. He's been a landmark for many of us, for longer than we can remember."

The woman sat down and contemplated the saint in front

of her,

"Well, you have done a good thing. I am sure many, many people have missed him being there."

Jimmy put his cap back on and busied himself with imaginary tasks.

"Have you had many visitors?"

Jimmy knew, from the shaky way she asked, that she was hoping for something.

"A few. I think you have been before? Matt was the first and then a man followed his dog here. I think he knew this guy here pretty well. They'll be back." He looked at his watch, "anytime now."

The blond stood up and made a show of checking her watch too,

"I need to go. Thank-you for the seat, and thank-you for saving St Anthony."

With a flash of blond hair she was gone, nearly tripping over Faithful as they both skirted the corner of the house.

Jimmy sat in her seat and fussed over the dog. A minute later, Tony appeared. Jimmy chuckled,

"I have just had a visitor who may or may not be the very person you wanted to see so desperately."

Tony stopped putting Faithful's lead on and waited for

Jimmy to continue.

"I didn't get her name so all I can tell you is what she looked like."

Tony closed his eyes,

"Blond, blue grey eyes and a nervous way about her."

Jimmy nodded. "So what's her name?"

"Christine. If it's really her."

Jimmy patted the feet of the statue and winked,

"See. I told you. I'm ninety-nine per cent sure that was the woman you're longing for."

Tony waved the comment away. He turned to Jimmy,

"So what about you? Why put a ruddy great statue here when you could have just let them dump it?"

Jimmy sighed,

"I think it all started with my dear mum. She's dead now. Eight years ago. I wasn't a good son. She was the best mother to me," he ran his the heel of his hand over his eyes, "but I did so much to push her away. She never stopped."

"Never stopped what Jimmy?"

Jimmy swore under his breath and angrily rubbed his eyes

again,

"Loving me."

The builder sat down on the bench.

"Can I make you a cuppa? Or something stronger?"

Jimmy shook his head,

"I stopped drinking a long time ago."

"Me too. Alcoholic father. Brother with many addictions which nearly killed him. So, how do you take your tea?"

"No sugar, no milk. Do you have the time?"

"I'm taking flexi for this. What about you?"

"We've reached the end of phase one. Just waiting for directions now."

Tony went into the kitchen, banged and clinked and emerged with two steaming cups of tea. If he saw the table already set for one or the stitched text on the wall he didn't let on.

"So, you were about to tell me about your mother?"

Jimmy took a sip of his tea,

"So it was always just me and her. Apart from when she brought a collection of waifs and strays she met either in church or on her way home. Sometimes people knocked on our door and she always let them in. She had a box of home-made biscuits and a freezer filled with scones so she was always ready. We had hardly any money, especially before I got a wage, but she always had those scones. At least, when I was there to notice. There was a dark time for a few years when I got in with the wrong crowd and drank too much. I only have vague recollections of that time. A lot of girls, a lot of dalliances. I don't think I could pick out any of them now. If I got any of them in trouble. they never told me. But then one night I came home and found mum crying. I knew it was because of me. Just knew it. From that time on, I gave up the drink, the parties, the crowd of no-gooders and the girls. I think I fought for the statue because of her. The memory of her opening her home to whoever needed it."

Tony wiped his eyes too,

"I wish I had met your mother. I could have used someone like her when I was a waif or a stray."

"She was the best human being I have ever known."

Tony lifted his mug and touched Jimmy's.

"To your mum and all like her,"

"And to St Anthony, who brought us together."

Tony

Tony hesitated at Jimmy's gate, which caused Faithful some consternation. He looked up and down the street. No sign of any visitors. He had to go to work. The days of sitting waiting and watching were no more. The days of sub-zero temperatures and near starvation were done. He had a steady income now. Nowhere near as much as before, but enough. He liked it that he knew exactly how much he had in his bank account and what he could spend. In his opulent days he just threw money away and never gave a thought to being without. And look what had happened then - total and utter desolation. Unemployment. Homelessness. Despair. Until two very different rescuers had turned his life around. Liz, the vicar had found him and brought him into the church. And Christine, she had given him hope again when he thought all was lost. It was not the time to reach out to her, as her violent now estranged husband turned out to be Gavin, his brother. Gavin had gone away and was busy building a better life for himself. He didn't know about Tony's dreams of giving his heart to Christine, but he had moved away from all that so hopefully…

When Tony arrived in work he walked straight into an

altercation between Patrick and Lisa. Patrick's face was pastier than usual and two red blotches had filled his cheeks. Lisa looked as though the whole situation was not phasing her at all.

"What's the problem here?"

Patrick stepped in front of Lisa,

"She wants me to increase her hours, and her pay. She's barely been in the job for a month. Ridiculous."

Lisa stepped round Patrick,

"I have spare time and my wage at the minute will not cover the bills. So I thought that solution would be to work longer and get more money. And my name," she nodded at Patrick, "is Lisa."

Tony pushed down his smile and nodded soberly,

"I don't see any reason for your request to be rejected. What do you think Patrick?"

Patrick spluttered,

"We can't just go round giving pay rises to whoever asks for them. There is a procedure for these things. A form."

Tony avoided Lisa's eyes,

"You are quite right Patrick. Find the appropriate paperwork and I will look over it myself. Lisa," Lisa jerked her head up, "you have to go through the right channels. We will try and help you but it can't happen straightaway. You know that, right?"

Lisa shrugged,

"Just thought there'd be no harm asking. Sorry if I went about it the wrong way."

"Well you did. And we will try and overlook that for you."

Tony could see the fury rising in Lisa's face,

"Well thank-you Patrick. Lisa, hopefully I'll sort that out for you. Don't be worrying."

Patrick made a noise that sounded like a scoff and walked away.

"Sorry Tony, I just thought I'd ask."

"It's fine. You asked the wrong person that's all."

They made a face at each other and went their separate ways.

Tony headed into his bare office and sat down. He contemplated his empty desk and sparse shelves. Other people had plants, folders and family photos, but he had nothing. There was a knock on his door. He looked up to see Jamie, the younger of the two boys he'd played football with many years ago. Jamie who was the spit of Gavin, but that must be his funny head again,

"Jamie! What are you doing here?"

The teenager took his mucky cap off and flushed,

"I was just looking for Lisa? There was no sign so I thought here would be the best bet. You're the manager here now?"

Tony smiled and hoped Jamie remembered him.

"Tony? Do you still have the dog?"

"Yes. Faithful is waiting at home for me."

Jamie looked off into the distance, remembering the dog, the church, the homeless man. He squinted at Tony,

"How come you're here now? What happened?"

"I got my act together and Simon (do you know him?) helped me get this job."

"Aw, Simon's great. He's Julie's boyfriend now. Did you know that?"

Tony leant back and gave in to incredulous laughter. As he dried his eyes he apologised,

"Do you ever feel that everything is connected? So many people in our wee corner of the world seem to know each other. Ah, here she is now."

Lisa came in and frowned at Jamie,

"This isn't my office. How did you end up here?"

Tony started to laugh again,

"Coincidence!"

Lisa shook her head,

"What's got into everyone today? Jamie, you should have asked for me in the kitchen, not marched into the boss's office!"

"I didn't see you down there and besides, me and Tony know each other from way back. He doesn't mind, do you Tony?"

Tony shook his head.

"Well, in future, Jamie, look harder for me."

Jamie shoved his hands in his pockets and gave a nod,

"Are you ready for that lunch you promised?"

"Yes. Let's go."

Jamie walked out and Lisa stood staring at Tony for a minute with a puzzled look on her face. Then she laughed and went after her son.

Tony looked at the closed door and thought about the two boys that Julie looked after but he'd gathered actually belonged to Lisa. Julie was their sister and Lisa was their mum. Who was their father? Whoever he was 'officially', Tony knew that Simon would make a better one. Someone who was actually present, not just a dream or a faint possibility. Tony had snatches of memories of his father. He had not been a bad man, just more away than there. And then he had dropped dead. A lesson about choosing life over work. Putting family above financial gain. Or, above drunken indulgence. Sadly, his brother Gavin had not learnt that lesson until he almost went the same way as their father with a heart attack. Hopefully now he had heeded the warning and made some drastic changes in his life. Maybe his weekly calls to Tony were one sign of that. His phone rang.

"Tony, it's Gavin. A quick question for you. You have a moment?"

Tony saw Patrick hanging around in the hall. He could hold his indignation for a bit longer,

"Yes. What is it?"

"I just heard from someone from my past. It's a long story but I just wondered, if you were given the chance to connect with a person (or two) who have been fine without you, would you?"

Tony thought of Christine,

"If you aren't causing them any hurt or stirring up things that should be left alone, then I don't see why not. You're not in trouble are you?"

Gavin gave a hollow laugh,

"Not really."

Tony rolled his eyes. How many skeletons did his brother have in his closet?

"Well then, I don't see any problem with reaching out. Don't tell me any more. I'll leave you to do it yourself."

Tony cleared his throat. It was now or never,

"How are things going with your new girl?"

"Slowly. I want to get it right this time."

"So, if you're happy now, I was wondering if I could get in touch with Christine?"

"Why?"

"Well, I've always wondered about her. How she is."

Gavin sighed loudly over the phone,

"I'm trying to re-build my life here. Could you not leave Christine alone?"

Tony's heart sank,

"Of course. Sorry."

He hung up. Tony set his phone down and put his head in his hands. So Gavin could walk away from the past, leaving it broken without a thought. He could only hope that this more recent connection Gavin was considering would fix something. Why had he said a person or two?

Were they connected? He shook his head. Not his problem. But Christine. How could he ever forget about her?

Matt goes back

Jimmy pulled his thick jacket closer round him. The sun was a whisper behind intermittent patches of grey and white cloud. But Jimmy was in the habit of drinking his tea on the bench outside now and a bit of early spring weather wasn't going to put him off. He looked over at St Anthony and was glad he had rescued him. What do you call someone who rescues a saint? A saviour of saints? A double hero? He held up three fingers and waggled the third one. He wondered how Matt was getting on with his search. Had he made progress or had he stopped and realised the goodness that was already there beside him? It took a few years for Jimmy to see the gift of his mum. He was ashamed of all those ungrateful, oblivious years. If you asked him what happened back then he couldn't have told you..

The gate creaked and in walked Matt. His face was clouded with a question.

"Well, hello again. I was just thinking about you. Any news?"

Matt sat down on the bench beside Jimmy and sighed.

"No. But I think my mum's been doing something."

"What makes you think that?"

"She keeps telling me not to worry, she's sorting it. Whatever 'it' means."

"That's good. Maybe? Do you have something to ask me?"

Matt started to jiggle his leg,

"I do. I did. But it's stupid."

Jimmy drained the last of his tea and waited. Matt cursed under his breath,

"When did you stop?"

"Stop what?"

"Looking for your dad. Wanting to know who he was, where he was, why he never showed up."

Jimmy took in Matt's flushed face and the bitter set of his mouth. He spoke with care,

"I never went out looking. I made stories up and sometimes lied to my schoolmates but that was it. I figured my mum had good reasons to keep him from me so even when I was older, I didn't give it a thought. If my dad knew he was my dad and still didn't come near me then he didn't deserve the name anyway." He reached out and put an uncertain hand on Matt's shoulder.

"That's all I've got for you son. I'm sorry there are no answers here."

Matt looked across at him then up to the statue. He sat with his head down. Jimmy left his hand on his shoulder. He felt his broken disappointment and had no words to help it. After a time Matt stood up,

"Any words of advice for me?"

Jimmy thought and shrugged,

"Just that it might help to look around you and see if maybe there's enough for you right here."

Matt nodded,

"You're right. I know you are. Hopefully I will be able to accept that soon."

The gate creaked again and Faithful crashed in, followed by a frustrated looking Tony. She jumped up at Matt straightaway who laughed and stroked her ears.

"I'm very sorry. It's a habit for her now. Every day, she turns out of the park and makes a bee-line for that statue. Sorry for the mad dog. Does she know you?"

Matt laughed,

"We met years ago but I think she's just friendly."

Tony's eyes were puzzled,

"We met that day too. We played football after my brother nearly had you for taking his watch?"

Tony scratched his head,

"Sorry, did you know my brother?"

"Nope."

Tony looked at Matt again,

"You sure?"

Matt laughed again,

"Yes. Never seen him before and never after either."

As Matt walked away Tony watched him go and shook his head. Jimmy took it all in and headed towards the kitchen,

"Time for tea?"

Tony followed him in. As they waited for the kettle to whistle he spoke again,

"That boy is the spit of my brother." He tutted at himself,

"My head is away today. Don't listen to me."

Jimmy poured the water into the orange teapot and said nothing. Then he clattered two teaspoons down on the counter. He peered out at St Anthony and was sure there was a smirk on his stone face. He sighed,

"I am beginning to regret having that wretched thing in my garden. Too many missing pieces are showing up and I don't have the strength to put them all together."

He covered his face. Now it was Tony's turn to put his hand on Jimmy's shoulder,

"What are you saying?"

Jimmy blew out his breath,

"That boy has been out looking for his father. I had nearly convinced him to be content with what he has already. And now you've made me wonder if you know him!"

Tony squeezed his new friend's arm,

"I have learnt to play the long game with these things. Let's keep that possibility to ourselves. We have no hard proof. Matt needs to learn that lesson for himself first."

Jimmy sighed,

"I suppose you're right. You didn't tell me anything. We're just having an innocent cuppa. And that fella out there has nothing to do with it."

"Well…"

"Ssh!"

Tony sipped his tea and stared into space. Jimmy did the same.

"You have any children Jimmy?"

Jimmy laughed,

"I know I said I didn't have the energy to put the pieces together but you don't need to step in."

"I didn't think I was. Sorry."

Jimmy drained his cup and wiped his mouth. He squinted over at Tony,

"I'm not a father, at least, no-one has told me otherwise."

"Me neither. It would have been nice, but disastrous if it had happened when I was in a mess."

Jimmy nodded,

"Maybe that's what happened with Matt's dad. He's out there, but it's just too complicated for him to step forward."

"Well he should have thought of that before then. Men are the worst, aren't they? Doing whatever and then walking away."

"No wonder there are so many fatherless. Including myself."

Tony stood then,

"I'd best be going now. Thanks for the tea. I'm sure

Faithful will make sure we meet again."

Jimmy watched him go and picked up the two cups. It had been a long time since he'd had more than one to wash. He had no memory of ever having anyone to drink tea with, since mum.

Matt and Simon

Simon had a day off. He left his empty house and walked to Julie's. He knew she was at work, but he'd rather sit in a place that was used to people than his bachelor pad. There was always a tiny hope that Matt or Jamie would be there, and he could try persuade them that he was a pretty nice person, really. He remembered hauling them out of the holiday Bible club when Matt was acting up. Matt. He sighed. So badly in need of a good dad. Simon sat on the couch and looked at his hands, remembering his mainly absent father. It was only in the past five years he had built a healthy relationship with him. Before that any memory he had was of his mum trembling when she saw her husband walking up the garden path, trying her hardest to keep him happy, enduring his harsh treatment of her. It had been so different when dad had come to live with him after his first heart attack. Eventually, they had fallen into a fairly pleasant way of going. And then he died. Simon let his tears well up and fall.

"Hey. Are you all right?"

He hadn't even heard Matt come in.

"Yeah. Just allergies."

"Right."

Matt sloped off to the kitchen. There was the sound of pans clattering and then sizzling. He came back with a plate of bacon and toast, setting it on the coffee table in front of Simon.

"You looked hungry."

Simon looked at the plate and couldn't speak.

"It would be better with a cup of tea. Give me a minute."

Matt disappeared again, giving Simon a chance to rub his face and process the kindness sitting in front of him. Where had that come from? He hoped it wasn't because Matt had done something wrong and wanted him on his side when he told Julie. When the tea came in, Simon raised his eyebrows at him,

"This is a first. You ok?"

Matt backed away,

"Yup. But you're not so…"

Simon tried to shake his head but Matt put his hand up,

"I know it's not allergies."

Simon blustered. Matt set the plate on his lap, put the tea close by and left the room. The toast was getting cold so

Simon made a buttie and ate. He sipped his tea, wondering how Matt had known he drank it hot and black. He didn't recall ever telling him. It was the result of too many weak, milky teas in the office over the years. Had Julie said, or had he been listening one time? He had most likely heard a lot more than he was old enough to hear. Certainly he had seen more than he should have. Imagine being brought up by your sister? Imagine never having an actual parent? Imagine never having a father. Simon thought back over the most recent years with his dad. He had made mistakes, but tried to make good in the end. Simon hoped he might have the chance to build a relationship with Matt. He didn't intend to walk away from this family, not like the others. They were here, he was here, and he intended to keep them close. He picked up his mug and plate. There was no time like the present.

Matt was not in the kitchen. Simon knocked on his chipped bedroom door and pushed it open over the worn carpet. Matt was sitting on his bed staring at the unopened letter in his hands. He started when Simon walked in, but made no move to hide. Simon crossed over and sat on the edge of the bed. He noticed that the quilt cover was a faded Liverpool one from a tournament dating back at least a decade ago.

"You ok?"

Matt lifted up the letter,

"This came for me and Jamie. I don't recognise the postmark or the handwriting."

Simon's heart sank,

"Do you think it's from your dad?"

Matt bit his lip and started to jiggle his leg,

"Maybe. I don't know whether to open it before Jamie's here, so I can prepare him, or just wait."

"What's your gut telling you?"

Matt paused,

"I've been searching, waiting for a long time. Jamie's happy to leave it. But - "

"You're not."

Matt shook his head.

"Sorry."

Simon stood up,

"I'm going to leave you to it. But, for what it's worth, anyone would be lucky to call you his son." Simon's eyes filled as he lifted his hand off Matt's back. If Matt saw it, he didn't let on. Simon walked away with stooped shoulders and slowly closed the door. Matt waited until the kitchen door opened and clicked closed again. He lifted up the envelope. If he was alive, what had kept him from showing up before now? Did he even know he had two sons? If he did, then why had he not appeared? Mum had been reluctant to tell him anything. Either she knew very little about the man who she had two kids with, or the real facts were too complicated to talk about. But he was officially an adult now. Definitely old enough to take it. Nearly as old as mum had been when she had him. Certainly older than when Julie was born. He thought back over the Christmases without any grown-ups. Or money. He patted his quilt, remembering the year she had got it for him. There had been offers to replace it. He didn't want any other. He'd keep it until it fell to pieces. It must have been so hard for Julie. He hadn't thanked her enough. He hoped she wouldn't be upset if their dad came into their lives for the first time. Or Simon.

Matt took a deep breath, shook his head and stuffed it in his pocket. It had been years, surely it could wait another day or two? Maybe he should give mum another chance to tell him herself or maybe Jimmy would tell him what to do? His advice had been good so far.

A new visitor

Jimmy traced his finger over the three names he had recorded. Matt had been back one more time to tell him he was trying to give the dad figure already in his life a chance. He seemed less troubled and more at ease now. Tony still appeared after Faithful every morning but was always looking over his shoulder when he was there. Christine had not been back. Jimmy gazed up at the statue,

"I don't think there is anything else for you to do here. Is there?"

Jimmy answered a persistent caller who he knew he was deliberately avoiding. He'd liked these quiet in-between days since the rubble had all been cleared and the boss had nothing for him to do. Once he answered this call, work would most likely start up again. He stared at the statue, mouthed thank-you and answered. He hung up a minute later and sighed; they demolished a beautiful building only to put up samey, pokey apartments in its place. Well, it paid the bills so that was that. Jimmy looked down at his hands, finally clean from builders' dust only to be made filthy again tomorrow. He worried about his three people coming when he was away. He hoped they would still come and sit on his bench, and get whatever they needed from that time.

As Jimmy walked with drooping shoulders back into the house he did not look back and realise it wasn't only the statue that helped people.

It was him too.

Liz leant against the car, shielded her eyes and peered at the statue. How on earth had it ended up in this middle-of-the-road estate? Was it not moved to a museum somewhere? What on earth use was it to anyone plonked on a random flower bed with no plaque or sign to say who he was? What he meant? She shook her head and marched up to the front door, ringing the doorbell before she had any second thoughts. There was a growing shape approaching her. Her heart started to thump. Why did she feel a strange dèja-vu coming over her? When he opened the door she remembered. His eyes widened too, as his past came back to him,

"Vicar?"

Liz smiled at him,

"Just Liz is fine. Sorry I can only remember your mum's name?"

"Yes, she was Nan. I'm Jimmy."

He stuck out his unusually clean hand and shook hers. They both stood at the door, not knowing what to say.

Jimmy cleared his throat and shoved his hands into his pockets.

"So, what brings you here?"

Liz pointed behind him to the statue,

"It took me a long time to find him, and then someone directed me here. I'm surprised, to be honest, that he wasn't claimed for the museum."

"They were going to dump him but something made me stop them."

Liz bit her tongue on all her theories and just smiled.

"Would you like a cup of tea?"

As she followed Jimmy into his kitchen, she glanced back at St Anthony and said a quick prayer into herself. It was only when the kettle whistled that she spoke,

"Your mum was always gathering people in. If she saw someone in need, she got alongside. Her scones, Jimmy, they were famous."

Jimmy nodded, his eyes filling. He moved over to make the tea and then rummaged in the bread bin, pulling out a bag and placing it on the table,

"Shop-bought I'm afraid."

Liz pulled one out and looked at it,

"Thank-you."

Jimmy sliced and buttered one, putting it on a chipped plate,

"Sorry I've no jam. Mum will be rolling over in her grave."

Liz took a bite and closed her eyes,

"She's not in her grave Jimmy, she is dancing in heaven over you."

This was too much. Jimmy stood up and turned away, blowing his nose.

"Jimmy, I know you've been through a lot, but you're doing a wonderful thing now."

She gave the burly man another moment to collect himself.

"So tell me, have you had many seekers?"

Jimmy frowned,

"Well, a few people have found him. And a dog."

"Was it Faithful and Tony?"

Jimmy laughed,

"I should have known you would have guessed them."

"Well, they were fairly regular attenders of the feet of the statue back in the day."

Jimmy nodded.

"Anyone else?"

"A young fella was here a few times. And one other…"

Liz looked at him,

"Think I can guess them too?"

"Probably."

Jimmy found himself holding onto his fourth finger.

"Was it Jamie? Because he has an interest in statues."

"No."

"His sister Julie?"

"Don't know them. No, it was Matt."

"Interesting. The quiet, serious brother."

"He wasn't really looking for the saint but he stopped anyway. Sat on the grass a couple of times."

"And did he leave happier?"

Jimmy shrugged,

"I never signed up for counselling duties. If he wants to

keep looking for his dad, who am I to stop him?"

"He has been searching ever since I've known him. I've never heard Julie wondering about hers."

"Is it the same person?"

Liz jerked her head towards him and contemplated him for a moment.

"I think Julie gave up on that a long time ago. She is more focused on building up what she really has right now?"

"And the other visitor? It wasn't Christine? If you saw Tony then Christine's never far behind."

Jimmy shook his head,

"You are a little creepy. Yes, Christine came to see the statue too. But she was definitely looking for somebody else. She never said who."

"So you've seen some of the people I have had my heart on for some time."

She took his hand,

"Thank-you for taking care of my statue, and some of my people."

She sighed, and said under her breath,

"I have always wondered whether God would make sense of you in the end."

Jimmy didn't hear. Liz stood up and took her cup over to the sink,

"Thanks for the tea Jimmy. I hope that saint over there brings you a few more lost souls."

Jimmy sighed,

"About that. I never really expected to actually have him long-term. My impulse was just to save him from the dump but now I'm seeing he is bringing more challenges than I realised."

Liz smiled and said nothing as she walked out the door, bowing once at the statue.

She turned, leaning on her stick,

"Keep it up, and I'll have a think for you. It's a heavy burden for you I know. The conversations I had with your mother all those years ago were no different. You've inherited her compulsion to help the lost Jimmy, whether you like it or not."

Jimmy stood taller as Liz left him. Finally he had meaning.

Julie joins the search

The flat door slammed.

"Do you know where he's taking himself off to every night?"

Simon lifted his hands,

"Beats me."

Julie put her fine blond hair into a thin pony tail and smoothed the bumps. She zipped up her Primark jacket and bent down to put her boots on.

"I've had enough of this wondering and worrying. By the looks of it, Lisa is leaving him to it."

She pulled her hood up and peered out the window into the rainy dark. Simon came and stood beside her,

"I have this recruitment event at the college tonight so I can't come with you. Sorry."

Julie turned to face him,

"I wouldn't have let you come anyway. The last thing Matt needs is a search party."

Simon put his arms around her,

"Just be safe. Most people out there are alright, but there are some bad eggs too. Don't stay out too long. And keep your phone with you."

"I'll be fine. Tougher than most."

Julie gave him a thumbs up and headed out.

Simon checked his watch. He had to leave in an hour. Hopefully she would be back soon. He sighed and rubbed his hand over his face. He had stepped into a difficult situation. But then. whose life didn't have complications in it?

She had forgotten her gloves and the rain was icy. Julie put her hands in her pockets, kept Matt's loping figure in her sights and walked into the wind. She could have waited for better weather but the curiosity was driving her mad. Matt's choice of direction was strange. She had expected him to head towards the offices near the river, the pubs behind them or the temporary shelters for the homeless. Why was he going up tidy streets with tiny gardens? Sure, most of the people who lived here were getting on. Too old to be his dad anyway. As she was looking in to the cheerily lit windows she lost sight of Matt. A wee fella met her stare and for a second they seemed to understand each other. There were two adults shouting in the room next to him. Julie put her lip out in sympathy. Maybe having a present but not welcome parent was worse than an absent one.

She kept on walking, hoping she would catch sight of her brother again. As she looked from side to side, a lit-up object caught her eye. It looked familiar. Where had she seen that before? Memories of a Bible club she had left her brothers to more than ten years ago, cleaning a messy church office and Liz, how could she forget Liz? A feeling of excitement propelled her through the gate. Matt was there, sitting on a bench as if he had been there before, talking to a man in builder's clothes like he was an old friend. Above them both was the statue of St. Anthony, glowing in the rainy dark. Julie hesitated. Matt looked happier than she had seen him in a long time as he chatted to this unknown man. She looked at them and had a warm feeling in her chest. They looked up and saw her, just smiling at them.

"Hi."

"What are you doing here?"

Matt's face was flushed with anger,

"You followed me."

Jimmy stood up and put his hand out,

"I'm the crazy fool that took this here statue. The name's Jimmy."

Julie laughed and shook his hand.

"So why did you follow me?"

"You've been disappearing a lot and I just wanted to check you were ok. No harm in that, is there?" She laughed and looked over to Jimmy for support. Matt tutted and rolled his eyes.

Jimmy noticed Julie's confusion and tried to change the subject,

"He's too big for my garden, I know. I'll try and find somewhere else soon. But he has brought a few people here that I'm glad I got to meet. Matt here, and now yourself, Julie." Jimmy nodded to her and glanced over at Matt.

"Matt was telling me about your friend Simon. Sounds like a good guy."

Matt glared at Jimmy. Julie put her shoulders back and lifted her chin,

"He is. One of the best. He's actually my boyfriend, so more than a friend. I've had my own share of trouble and Simon has been my rock."

Matt looked quickly at Julie, like he had forgotten who she was.

"Yeah, Jimmy, Julie is officially my sister. Mum has been around sometimes, but it's mainly Julie."

Jimmy glanced at Julie,

"So you have the same dad as Matt?"

"No. I've never known who he was, and to be honest, I've never wondered either. Mum wasn't clear on the details, so I just moved past it. Maybe you need to do that too Matt?"

Jimmy looked from one to the other,

"I've been trying to say that to him as well."

Matt waved their ill-considered advice away,

"I'm not like you two: either making up lies about your dad, or pretending he never existed. I want the truth. You can't stop me."

With that, Matt stormed off, leaving Jimmy and Julie staring after him.

"He'll cool down soon and realise that Simon is a better version than anyone."

Julie crossed her hands over and brought them in to her chest,

"I really hope so. So you never knew your dad either?"

"Nope. It wasn't a big loss for me. Maybe if he'd been there, I wouldn't have gone off the rails twenty odd years ago. That time is lost to me. Just a haze of drink and faces I don't recall. I hope Simon pulls Matt back from all that."

Julie looked at Jimmy and tilted her head to one side,

"Who pulled you back?"

"My mum. I think you will help Matt too. Fathers aren't the only superheroes you know."

Julie wiped a cuff over her eyes and turned her face to him,

"Not all mums are as great as yours though."

"But what about sisters? Now, they can be the secret weapon," Jimmy winked at her.

Julie gave a watery laugh,

"We do our best. So do you have any memory of that time?"

Jimmy stood up and beckoned her to shelter under his back porch,

"I keep hoping that something will trigger it. I sometimes feel that I've missed an important part, but who knows"

He looked down to see Julie's hand on his sleeve. It gave his heart a jolt. She smiled up at him,

"I need to go but thanks for being there for Matt. Maybe we'll be back with good news one day."

With that, Julie ran off, dodging the puddles like a little girl. Jimmy watched her and said to himself, or to the Saint beside him,

"Someone, somewhere, has missed being a father to that angel."

The spotlight on the statue flickered and Jimmy froze.

"

Matt gets one answer

Matt was sitting on his bed staring at the unopened letter when Jamie flung open their door,

"What's that? Who's it from? Anything exciting?"

Matt put the letter beneath his leg,

"No. I'll check later. Probably just the college wanting more money or something."

Jamie accepted the answer.

"You're home early today?"

Jamie pushed back the curtain and revealed the tipping rain,

"No-one can work in that. The soil is a mud bath, the plants are submerged and even the boss has headed home."

Jamie had taken on a part-time job when he had any free periods at school.

"But you're liking it, right?"

"I love it. Being outside, apart from days like today, is the best."

Matt touched the envelope beneath him and heard himself asking it,

"Jamie, do you ever think about our dad?"

Jamie frowned,

"Which one are you talking about? The one we'll probably never meet, an imaginary one or Simon?"

"Simon's not our dad."

"He's closer to being it than anyone."

Jamie sighed,

"To be honest, I try not to think. I went through that strange time when I lied about it but now I find getting a spade in my hand and digging helps put any thoughts away. Maybe you should try it. Instead of pounding the streets to nowhere every night."

Matt's jaw clenched,

"I'll have you know that I've found someone and something that might interest you, if you'd ever think of asking."

Jamie rolled his eyes,

"Who? What?"

Matt stood up, annoyed.

Jamie snatched at the envelope that Matt had left in full view on the bed. He shook his head,

"What have you done Matt?"

The younger brother did not hesitate to tear into the letter. He read the sparse lines shaking his head. Matt held his breath. All his hopes were right there, on that bit of paper. Jamie tossed it over to him and folded his arms. Matt read it and re-read it. Crumpling it up, he left the room, banging straight into Simon. He pushed him to one side and raged out the front door.

Simon looked after him but left him to it. He knocked on the boys' door and found Jamie sitting on his bed, looking at the floor. Simon leant against the wall,

"Everything all right here? I know it's none of my business so you don't need to tell me." He shrugged and pushed off the wall to leave again.

"No Simon, wait! It was just a letter from our dead-beat so-called father, signing off on having anything to do with our lives. I don't care. He has never been a father to either of us so why would he start now? I know Matt had built this up but he's not seeing things right."

Simon held his breath as Jamie kept talking,

"He doesn't see yet that you are the best person we have right now, apart from Julie."

"I love being your person, Jamie. The term 'dad' is overrated, don't you think?"

Jamie hugged him in a back-thumping way,

"You never know Simon. Give it time."

Jamie headed out to the library and Simon mulled over his words.

Meanwhile Matt was storming through the pelting rain, letting it beat against his shoulders and soak his back. He didn't care. He sped up as the statue caught his eyes. He ran the last part and knocked on the door. He hadn't noticed the car wasn't in the drive. He knocked again and pressed the doorbell. He cursed and kicked the door. No-one was home. He went through the gate and sat down on the seat beside the statue anyway. He looked over the paper that had taken what little hope he'd had left and then dropped it on the seat beside him. That was it then. 'Nice to know you are getting on well. Keep it up. Gavin.' It wasn't hard to remember, but he wished he could forget. He wished there had never been a letter. That way he could have kept making excuses. The hard truth of it was, his 'dad' wanted nothing to do with him. Or Jamie. Matt picked up a stick and threw it at the statue. The face did not change from its kind expression. Hot rage welled up from Matt's stomach and he let it take over. It was only when he had thrown the brick that he came to his senses and ran away.

Tony figures something out

"Not again Faithful!" Tony had hoped for a quick walk this time. It was late and it was raining. But, like clockwork, Faithful had turned and made an irrefutable beeline to the statue. Tony sped up after her, pulling at his hood to keep at least a bit of the water off him. His head was down so he nearly crashed into someone running the other way.

"Watch it mate!"

The figure kept running. Tony started to call after his dog again and turned into Jimmy's garden. This time Faithful had something in her mouth and was growling at the scene in front of her. Someone had thrown something at the statue and one of his hands was knocked off. Tony prised the thing out of Faithful's teeth and sat down to look at it. He read the crumpled letter and looked at the broken hand. There was a sad story here, he could see it. Jimmy's headlights bounced off Tony and he was there beside him, standing shaking his head at what he saw,

"I know it wasn't you, but did you see who was here before?"

"No. I might have bumped into him on my way but didn't get a good look at him because of the rain."

Jimmy pointed at the bit of paper,

"Is that a clue?"

Tony handed it over. Jimmy read it and shook his head sadly,

"So I think I know the broken heart who did this."

"I think I do too."

They both looked at each other and said the name at the same time,

"Matt."

Jimmy picked up the stick and the bits of marble on the grass.

"I've been wondering for a while now…"

Jimmy turned from picking moss off the statue,

"About what?"

Tony cleared his throat, started to speak and then shook his head,

"This is ridiculous. I haven't even, I have never, I should have checked with him before."

The rain had got heavier as Jimmy's insistence increased,

"What is it Tony? It's only me here, and I'm not the type to gossip."

Tony tugged at his hood and headed over to the small shelter above Jimmy's door. Jimmy ran to stand beside him, not wanting to break the spell by searching for his door key. Faithful was pawing at it now.

"You may as well come in away from that soaking."

Jimmy opened the door and flicked the light on. Faithful pushed past him and sat plonk on the linoleum. Tony followed and hesitated,

"I'm not 100% sure, but I think Matt and Jamie's father is my brother."

Jimmy pulled out a chair and sat down with care.

"And where is he now?"

"Across the border, Newcastle."

"So he used to be local?"

"Yup. We both grew up here. Our parents are dead. We went our separate ways. Gavin got married. But he hasn't had the greatest track record. Drink and all the vices that are connected with it sent him a dangerous way."

Jimmy nodded like he had been that way once or twice

too.

"I'll need to check all this out with their mother before I say anything more."

"Do you know her?"

"Yes. Slightly. Do you?"

Jimmy gave one shake of his head and drew his eyebrows together.

"I don't think so. But I couldn't say for certain."

Tony nodded,

"We all have our hazy pasts."

Jimmy put his head down and then jerked it up,

"If you have a suspicion you know that you owe it to Matt to pursue it."

The light on St. Anthony flickered outside the window then.

"I think, Tony, it's time for you to live up to your namesake."

Tony sighed and stood up,

"I wonder what possessed my mother to burden me with that name!"

"And I wonder why the memory of mine made me rescue that thing in my garden!"

Both men looked out at the saint and fell silent.

"What happened to her?"

"Who?"

"You said your brother was married?"

Tony looked at his watch,

"He was. But not any more. I need to get going."

"You're going to find all that out for Matt, aren't you?"

"I'll do my best."

Tony clicked Faithful's lead on and made for the door.

"Tony? His wife wasn't the blond that showed up here?"

Tony was gone before Jimmy got an answer. But he was left confused. That was one connection too far wasn't it? He looked out at the lit-up saint and laughed. After a life of feeling alone, this was getting quite crowded now. There was another thing but he'd put that to the back of his mind. Sometimes, lost things were better off staying that way. He turned his back on the statue with that thought. He went back into the garden and picked up the broken off hand. He held it and glanced over at the keeper of lost things,

"You can keep secrets too can't you?"

He headed back in with the hand, meaning to get glue for it tomorrow. Once he had fixed it, he'd phone Liz. She would know what to do. Liz always knew. The secrets she must have heard over the years. Did she even know his?

The hiding ones

Tony pressed the buzzer he guessed belonged to Lisa's flat. A young girl was walking in increasingly tighter circles with a screaming pram. Lisa's curtain twitched as she looked to see who was there. She waved at Tony and buzzed him in.

Tony pushed the open door to her flat and found her frantically throwing empty fast food boxes into the corner of the kitchen.

"Don't be tidying up for me. Sure you've seen where I used to live."

Tony screwed up his face and then sat on the sofa, pulling up a crumpled takeaway menu from under him.

"What are you doing here? Have I lost my job? Was it Patrick? I honestly thought I was working pretty well there."

Tony waved her panic away,

"No, everything there is fine. I just had a pretty huge

question for you."

He pinched the bridge of his nose and spoke into his hand,

"Those boys, Matt and Jamie, they're yours right?"

Lisa sat on the chair opposite him,

"I thought I told you that already."

Tony let out a long breath,

"I think I've worked out who the father is. You obviously know."

He laughed, "You were there."

Lisa put her hands together between her knees. She was biting her lip.

"So who is it then?"

Tony frowned at her,

"I'm not sure that you know this part, but is it my brother, Gavin?"

Lisa cursed,

"I didn't know he was your bleeding brother!"

Tony shrugged,

"We aren't that close so that's why it took me so long to

figure it out."

Lisa stood up,

"We had a strange off-on thing. He would look me up from time to time and we'd carry on where we'd left off. Sometimes I thought we had something, but I should have known then he disappeared both times I told him I was pregnant. He never had me round to his place, never left a toothbrush in mine."

Tony sighed. She grabbed his arm,

"He sent money. He wasn't the worst."

Lisa was shaking and pulling at her sleeves,

"You must think I'm a waste of space. See, I didn't have anyone to tell me how to live. I was, am, a mess. Just lost."

She put a fist in her mouth to stop the sobs.

"And you know that Gavin wrote a letter recently?"

Lisa shook her head,

"I asked him to reach out but I didn't know he had."

"He did. But it was nowhere near enough for Matt. He left it on the bench opposite the statue in that garden up yonder."

"What statue? What garden? Why was he even there? And how do you even know all this?"

Tony laughed,

"You can thank the dog for that. She led me to the statue, the garden, the man who lives there and the letter."

Lisa swore again.

"Did you know the man?"

"No, but I do now."

"I need to see Matt. Sorry, Tony, I have to go."

She put her hand up,

"Show yourself out and don't follow me. Today is not the day for the boys to discover they have an uncle. Soon, just not now."

Tony sat down on another menu and shook his head,

"I'm an uncle. I had not thought of that."

He sat for a long time, trying to process it all. So that day when he thought he had just come across Gavin and was holding him off the boys, they were actually his *sons*. But they had not known that either. He and Lisa must have met when Gavin was already with Christine. At least when Jamie was thought of. He sighed and closed his eyes. What a mess. When it all got back to Christine, it would destroy her. But she would work it out eventually, one way or another. He put his head in his hands and groaned, his brother had done some terrible things. Is that what happened when you had no-one to guide you? It should have been him. He should have stopped it. All of it. What had been doing during that time? Just working, reaching for more status, more money. Those were his heady glory days before he stretched too high and it all came crashing down.. If only he had stayed closer to his brother, he could have stopped him. He could have ended the cycle before young fatherless boys were created. Before Christine's life was utterly ruined. He gave a hollow laugh. There was sharing the name of a saint and actually being one. He wondered how many people and hearts had been lost because of his brother, and if you follow it back, because of him. He, Tony, was not the saint who found lost things. he was the wastrel who let them scatter.

Tony stood up, brushed the old crumbs off his trousers and, after a sorrowful look at the hovel his friend called home, he left.

Lisa was walking slowly up the street, peering through every side gate, scanning the tops of privet hedges, searching. She stopped to smooth her wild hair and straighten her denim jacket. For some crazy reason, she felt that this was a significant moment, deserving of a tidy appearance. And then she saw him. It was the same statue that she used to stumble towards with her drinking buddies. Who knew where any of them were now. Some were probably dead. There was one night she remembered, but the face she wanted to put with it was long gone. But wait! There was Matt and he was standing beside the very person she had been trying to remember for such a long time. She ducked. Neither of them had seen her. She would have gone in if it was just Matt but…

Lisa ran, her breath coming out with every slap of her foot against the concrete. She squeezed her eyes tight against the face of the man she had thought was lost to her. The one who she had half-heartedly searched for all those years ago. The reason she had worn the badge of single mother for. She had always thought he was either dead or oblivious to her. If Julie knew, what would she do to her? Just when they were starting to be ok with each other. She should have known this knotted mess would pull her back in.

"Wait! Stop! Please!"

She turned to see the face approaching her, Matt close behind. She turned.

"Lisa! Is it really you?"

Lisa's arms dropped to her sides. She shook her head and made Matt her focus,

"You ok son? Took me a while to find you. That statue, eh? There's no escaping it."

Matt looked at the man and then his mum.

He shrugged,

"So you found me. What's the matter?"

Lisa gave a nervous laugh,

"I heard that your father contacted you."

She rubbed the sides of her legs,

"Was it ok?"

Matt frowned,

"What's it to you? And how did you know anyway?"

Another nervous laugh,

"I just hear things, you know."

Matt pointed a shaking finger at her,

"Did you ask him to? It was out of the blue…"

Lisa shook her head. It wouldn't help if he knew.

"Well it was crap. No point in it. So that's it. My dad's dead. To me at least."

Lisa put her head down. Matt slammed the gate behind him. It bounced back. Jimmy looked at Lisa as the memory of her rushed back. He had to know.

"Lisa? Are you here for anything else?" Lisa let out a long sigh and stumbled over to the statue, putting her hands on him. She looked sideways at Jimmy,

"I thought you were dead. Sorry I didn't try to find you. I didn't know for a while. I hoped it would just go away. But it didn't."

Jimmy watched Lisa wipe her face and waited. She

whispered,

"I called her Julie."

Jimmy put his hands in his pockets and chewed the inside of his cheek.

"I know. I met her her a week ago. I didn't know then that she was, is she, my daughter?"

The tears were running down both their faces.

"There was no-one else back then, so she must be yours."

"I'm sorry. For never looking for you. For not letting you…"

"Be a father? I was a mess back then so probably a blessing you never found me."

"Until now. You don't seem to be bad anymore?"

Jimmy sighed and glanced up to the statue. No thunder bolts there. He wandered over and perched at the base of the saint. Lisa looked at him and laughed,

"if I had any doubts it was really you, they're gone now. You look the same, just a bit older."

Jimmy pulled a face,

"But a lot has changed since then."

Lisa sighed and sat on the bench close by,

"For us both. What's happened for you all this time?"

Jimmy wished he had smokes on him. He patted his empty pockets anyway,

"I gave up all that drinking nonsense, went back to me mam, nursed her until she passed. She never knew she was a granny. Just as well, maybe."

Lisa started picking at the grass. She had never known her granny and her mum had died when she was pregnant with Matt.

"So, will you tell her?"

"Who?"

"Julie."

"Tell her what?"

"That I'm her dad. Sort of."

Lisa scrubbed her face with both hands and dropped them to shrug.

Jimmy's face fell then he recovered himself,

"You're right. What would be the point now?"

He patted his trousers again,

"Oh for a smoke."

Lisa watched him. He met her eyes,

"I never knew my dad. Matt is a mess because *his* dad doesn't want to know him. But I'm here. No plan to go anywhere. It mightn't be such a bad idea?"

Lisa was searching her pockets now.

"Let me think about it."

With that, she nodded to him and to the statue before walking away.

Jimmy whistled. He looked at St Anthony.

"Enough now. Who knew that finding things could be so hard?"

Closer to home

Matt grunted up from his bed,

"What now?"

Jamie dropped down on his legs.

"Ow! Get off!"

His younger brother stood up again,

"Just wanted to say I'm sorry the letter was not what you'd hoped for."

Matt sat up so he could shrug his shoulders,

"Doesn't matter. He's a waster. At least we know that now."

Jamie flushed,

"Wanna know that I think?"

"Not really but go ahead."

He started walking round the room, running his hand along the bumpy wall.

"Remember when I stole that prodigal thing and hid it under my bed?"

Matt grunted again.

"Well, I started thinking then about dads, and how they can be anyone. Dads can be our mum, or mums can be our dad or whatever."

Matt held back his laughter and let Jamie carry on. Jamie coughed,

"Back then it made me feel better when I thought that I could find everything I needed right here, close by. I mean, Julie has done nearly everything for us. And now there's Simon."

"Speaking of…Here's the man himself."

Simon stood at the door, hesitating.

"I just wanted to say I'm sorry about the letter too. And maybe, some day, I could try to help in some way. I'm not much good at football, but there's got to be other ways…"

Matt nodded.

"There may be. We'll see."

Jamie glared over at him,

"We don't even know what a 'dad' is supposed to look like or do. That's what I'm trying to say."

Matt rolled his eyes,

"And do we even need that? We've got along just fine until now, haven't we?"

Simon looked at his watch,

"Well, it's nearly dinner time. Want to go out and get a burger? I'll text Julie so she can meet us there."

Matt and Jamie left to get their jackets and shoes, trying not to think that this was exactly what a dad would do. Jamie straightened his grin and Matt avoided anyone's eyes.

When they got seats in the burger joint down the hill just along from St Anthony's, they all looked round them. The place was full of couples and family groups. Jamie caught himself staring at the 'normal' family of dad, mum, son and daughter. They were laughing at something and seemed happy. At the next table was a group of teenagers. And then a young man and a small boy. The older one was looking down at his phone, and the boy was struggling with his Transformer toy. He kept looking up at the man but he didn't seem to notice. Jamie made to get up but an arm stopped him,

"Just leave it."

Jamie hissed back,

"But I can help him."

A young greasy looking girl came over to take their order then, and the boy left with his adult. Jamie could not accept he was the dad. Surely a more invested person would have noticed the wee fellla needed help? Turning his back away from Matt, Jamie saw his chance when the man went up to pay.

"Hey! I can show you how to transform it if you like?"

Jamie put his hand out and the boy hesitated.

"Don't be shy."

When the boy handed it over, and Jamie was about to twist it back, the man came over,

"What do you think you're doing? Give that back and get away from my brother!"

Jamie clicked it into car shape and passed it over,

"Sorry, I just thought I could show him how to do it. You seemed, er, busy."

The man seemed to deflate all of a sudden. When the wee boy had moved away a bit, he said in a low voice,

"He lost his dad two months ago and I was just taking him out to give his mum some space. I was on my phone because we're trying to find somewhere else for them to live. Too many memories where we are now."

Jamie sucked his breath in,

"I'm sorry about your dad. And I'm sorry for interfering."

"He wasn't my dad. He was just my neighbour. My dad is alive and well. My name's Will by the way."

Jamie stuck his hand out,

"I'm Jamie and this is Matt, my brother, and Simon."

If Simon had wanted a title, or noticed the absence of one, he didn't bat any eyelid. The two boys left, the taller bending down to hold the younger one's hand. As they watched them go Matt nudged Jamie,

"See? You of all people should know that things are never what they seem."

They all left then, tipping the waitress who hadn't really deserved a tip but the burgers had been good and she'd brought them through on time.

"Well, thanks Simon."

The three walked to Simon's car, thinking about Julie, and wondering where she was. Surely she should be finished for the day. What was she at now? Not wanting to look like he was just the 'boyfriend', Simon had not picked up his phone in front of the boys. If he was worried, he tried hard to hide it.

Matt said it out loud first,

"Where's Julie? She doing a late shift today?"

"Don't ask me. I'm not her keeper. Simon?"

Simon shrugged,

"Something must have come up. I'm as in the dark as you."

Jamie stopped at the car,

"Should we go look for her?"

Matt shook his head,

"Let's just go back and wait at home. Where would we go anyway?"

"Where you have been disappearing to every night. Where the statue is."

Matt blew out his breath,

"I didn't know you knew anything about that. But it doesn't explain why Julie would go there."

Simon looked from one to the other across the roof of the car. Matt was already towering above him. Jamie wasn't far off. But somehow he knew they were in need of a father figure. Taking them for a burger was not the same thing. He got in the car with slumped shoulders. Jamie's hand landed on one of them.

"Thanks dad."

Matt said nothing. Simon sniffed the whole way home.

Julie is not looking

Julie wasn't sure why she was headed up the hill again. Work was done and she knew there had been rumblings about dinner out tonight but still her feet were taking her the same way Matt had been this past while. Somewhere in her mind she wondered if the saint had anything to do with it. How could he? A statue of stone had no power over anything. When she got near, a grey head appeared over the hedge and she wondered if he was somehow involved.

She heard raised voices and stepped behind one of the higher hedges. It was the same window she had looked in before. The same boy stood there with his hands over his ears while the same two adults shouted at each other in the room next door. If she had seen this the only two times she had passed by, it must happen a lot. Her heart hurt seeing it. How much more pain did she have to encounter? She stepped out again and kept on to her destination, if that was what it was. The gate was open today because he was sweeping the path. She hesitated and stood still.

"Come on ahead, Julie, is it?"

Julie tucked her hair behind her ear and half-smiled.

"Matt isn't here today, if you were looking for him?"

Julie shook her head,

"I know where he is. I don't really know why I'm here, to tell the truth."

Jimmy looked at her nose and her ears. Only one other person he knew had those features. Him. He smiled at Julie,

"Well, it's nice to see you here anyway. Tea?"

"No thanks."

She sat on the edge of the bench and gave a cough.

"Did you ever know my mum, Lisa, say about twenty years ago?"

Jimmy sat on the other end of the seat and started to rub his thighs,

"Maybe. That time is a bit hazy though."

"Have you seen her recently? Did you talk?"

Jimmy knew he was heading for uncharted waters. He looked up at the statue and prayed for kindness.

"Sorry, too many questions. I blame Matt; he's been

searching for a long time. Must have rubbed off on me."

Julie gave a laugh and started to leave. Her arm was touched,

"Don't go. I think you might be my…"

Jimmy took a breath and said the truth he'd wondered about for many years,

"I think I'm your dad."

Julie stopped and faced him. There was no surprise in her face, just fury,

"Why are you only telling me this now? Did it never dawn on you that I may have needed you years ago, when I was left alone to figure life out all by myself? Because she did leave me alone. A lot. I skipped school, I hid from the social services, I brought up my brothers. I survived on the money posted through the letterbox but I never knew when that would happen, I did without food so they wouldn't have to, I held my head up when everyone else seemed to have everything I didn't."

She dropped to the bench and let the beginning of twenty years worth of tears begin to fall. Jimmy stood watching her with nothing to say. His hands were clenching and unclenching.

He eventually sat beside her.

"We both had far too much that night- to drink, to smoke, everything. I can hardly remember it."

Julie tutted as Jimmy kept speaking,

"She never told me. Yesterday was the first time. I had no idea. I'm sorry."

Julie rubbed her face and stood up.

"I need to go."

She stopped at the gate,

"I've got along just fine without you. I realised a long time ago that families, fathers, the whole lot, are a fantasy for most. A dream that needs to be let go of so we can get on with living whatever life we've got."

Jimmy felt her sadness hitting him and took his punishment. He held onto the fence and watched her go. The daughter he never knew he had. That his mum would never know. Or had she known more than him, back when life was hazy? He would never know.

His kitchen seemed more empty when he stepped back inside. The usual single setting that had not bothered him before was mocking him now. When he lifted the lid of his weekly dinner, the smell turned his stomach. How had he been eating this, day in day out for years? He rattled in the drawer for a ladle, opened the lid of the bin and began to spoon the contents of the pot into the bin. He looked down at the rejected food and pressed his lips together. Why had he put up with this for so long? He lifted the bag and tied the ends, heading straight outside to dump it into the landfill bin. Looking over at the saint, he shook his head,

"You do not belong there. Definitely not."

So what on earth was he going to eat now? He lifted down the old binder his mum had referred to many times when she had been planning the dinners every night. Just holding it brought her back. The cover was stained with the cooking and baking she had done over the years. He undid the elastic band keeping it all together and notes in mum's neat writing slipped onto the table. The one on top was not a surprise. As Jimmy read over the simple list of ingredients, a crazy idea came to him. He said the items out loud as he put his coat on, grabbed his wallet and got into his car. The local shop would definitely have them all.

It did. Jimmy carried the bag into his house and turned the oven on. That was one thing he remembered from his mum. He lined up the flour, sugar, eggs and butter. There were very few instructions on the page. One line just read, 'put into the oven and bake.' He closed his eyes and tried to picture his mum baking.

"Well, there's only one thing to do."

He measured the butter and flour and started mixing it with his fingers. At least the way he vaguely recalled mum doing. He added the sugar and looked at the egg. Shrugging his shoulders he broke it on top of everything else and stirred it round. He dumped the mix out on the counter and looked at it. He made a face at his hands, rubbed them clean on a towel and went looking for a cutter. When he couldn't find one he started to make scone-like piles and put them on a tray. They looked almost ok. He put them in the oven and sat down to watch, flicking through the cookbook while he waited. He turned over a couple of lists of ingredients and then stopped. This was not just a list of recipes, his mum had used the pages to write other things down. They weren't letters or plans. They looked like prayers? As he read some, he realised that his name was in them all. *Dear Lord, help my lost son Jimmy. He has gone his own way, and only You can bring him back.*

They were nearly all the same. Jimmy lifted up page after page of his mother's heartache. He searched for a date, but had to guess instead. The handwriting was neat at the start but seemed to lose its way as the prayer became scribbled and more frantic. He sat back and sighed. What pain he had put her through. If only he had come home sooner. She could have shown him how to make edible scones, not the dubious burnt heaps he had just pulled out of the oven. Who would know what he had done wrong? Well, taking them out sooner would be a help. He lifted one and tried to cut the flat lump in two. He smeared butter on a thin part of it. His mum would have been able to see what was missing straightaway. He bit into it and made a face, looking out at Liz standing having an intent conversation with the statue. How long had she been there and what on earth was she doing here anyway? He knocked on the window and beckoned her in.

"You need to mix in some milk too. And get a cutter."

She set down his attempt and glanced over at the cook book pages, scattered over the kitchen table,

"Good. I told her to write them down,.."

"You knew?"

Liz smiled with her lips closed.

"How?"

Liz lifted up a scone and set it down again.

"Your mum was at church every week, so I got to know her, over many years. She was always talking about you Jimmy."

Jimmy put his head down,

"I brought her a lot of trouble."

"Which is why I encouraged her to put some of it down on paper."

Jimmy walked over to the window,

"What were you saying to him just there?"

Liz laughed and tapped the side of her nose,

"Can a vicar not keep her own secrets? One thing I will tell you is, use self-raising flour the next time."

With that, she left. Jimmy put his hands on his hips and surveyed the mess.

"The next time?! She's having a laugh!"

Who is the real father anyway?

Simon sighed as he looked at the calendar. It was Father's Day. Was that a day for all official dads, or could some wannabes get under the line too? He did think he'd ticked most boxes that people linked to fatherhood. The real test lay with the boys. He might never know of course. Like he had no clue if his other idea would be welcomed or not. He jumped when he heard Julie crashing through the front door and quickly put his plan back into his jacket.

"Well, hello. Guess what?"

Simon stood up and gave Julie a kiss,

"What?"

"I met my real dad yesterday."

Simon sat down abruptly. Julie sat beside him and told him the whole story, or as much as she and Jimmy knew.

"I'll have to speak to mother of course."

"But you haven't yet?"

Julie shrugged and rolled her eyes.

"That's a fairly significant conversation."

"That can wait, as it has done for years."

Simon knew better than to say anymore. Matt came through the door.

"No classes today?"

"I had one this morning and that's it. Jimmy, you know him, well he has invited me and all of you round to his for something to eat tomorrow late afternoon. He did say what but I can't remember now."

Julie flushed but said nothing.

"What does 'all of you' mean?"

Matt put his hands up,

"I think he meant me, Jamie, Julie and you Simon, but he maybe he meant mum too?I know he's met her."

Julie had a coughing fit and had to leave the room. Simon followed her,

"I bet you Liz has something to do with this too. She's always trying to get people together. You remember that crazy Christmas when she got Lisa and Tony round? This is just like that."

Julie straightened the chairs,

"I need more time. I've had enough of people landing into my life before I'm ready. This," she waved her hand round the room, "is all I need. Life hurts when you let more people in."

"You let me in though. I hope that hasn't brought you pain."

Julie shook her head,

"You're different."

"Jimmy might be ok. If you go there and you don't like it, you can walk away and that can be the end of it. I'll be right beside you."

Simon felt the shape of the ring in his pocket and his heart sank. If this change was too much for Julie, then proposing another one would be poor taste. He excused himself. He stood in front of the bathroom mirror and made a face at himself. What on earth did he have to offer this amazing, courageous, resilient woman with her upside down family? Maybe this Jimmy person would be all she needed? All that the boys needed. He put his hands on either side of the sink and sighed. Then he straightened up, pulled a smile at himself and walked out.

Julie frowned at him,

"You ok?"

He smiled again,

"Of course. Never better."

Julie leant in and put her arms around him,

"You know I couldn't do all this without you."

"You managed before."

"Barely. I was so alone, struggling. I felt abandoned. There was no-one to turn to. No-one to talk to. Before you. You made everything so, so much better."

Simon looked down and waved the praise away.

"I mean it. You changed everything."

****
****

Matt was standing in the hall in their house and had been about to go in but he stopped himself and went out instead. He still didn't know how Simon being around all the time made him feel. He headed to Lisa's. He hesitated on the doorstep. She might still be at work but you never know..

There was no answer, even after pressing the buzzer three times. A woman came out the main door and Matt caught it before it closed. He took the steps two at a time, not thinking about why he was rushing when she wasn't in. Or was she? Her door opened and Matt stepped back into the shadows.

"Well thanks, Lisa. I'll hopefully see you next Wednesday?"

Matt waited until the noise of footsteps had faded before he moved out of his hiding place. What was that vicar doing at his mum's flat? And what was mum at, letting her in? He had never wanted to see her again, after the incident at Bible club but then she showed up with that turkey on Christmas Day of all times and stayed for most of the day! Who does that? He knocked on Lisa's door, shaking his head at all these food-orientated gestures. Christmas Dinner and scones, what did food have to do with it? His mum opened the door. Her eyes looked bloodshot.

"Oh hi Matt. No college today?"

Why was everyone interested in his timetable all of a sudden?

"Why are you not at work?"

"I had today off. Liz paid a visit. I'm surprised you didn't run into her there."

Lisa opened the door wider and Matt followed her in. He sat down and the question burst out of him,

"So how many men did you hook up with over the years?"

"Only two."

"And you made them both fathers. What were you

thinking?"

Lisa's eyes filled,

"I wasn't the first time. The next one was more steady and I hoped he would stay. So we could be a family, you know?"

Matt scoffed,

"How wrong you were. He never wanted you, me or Jamie."

Lisa rubbed her legs and managed to whisper,

"You don't know that. Maybe, something happened."

"Like he already had a wife and you were just a bit on the side."

Lisa shook her head,

"No. He just, he wasn't good at settling down that's all."

"And still you decided twice, not once, to force his hand and bring two boys into this life without ever having a dad. Well done Lisa. Well bleeding done."

Matt stormed out. Lisa covered her face and sobbed. Today had been a day of facing up to all of her mistakes. Matt hadn't realised he wasn't the first to get at her today. She thought over what had just happened with Liz. She had not realised how much Liz and Nan had known about her and Jimmy's antics back then.

You and your pals were oblivious to the people watching your comings and goings that day. But there was no avoiding the racket you made, especially when there was a church service going on. You all liked to sit around the statue which riled all the stuffy ones in the church. We both saw how young you were, but there was no-one to tell you otherwise and it certainly was not our place. So we just watched as you and Jimmy spent more and more time together. And then, after a few weeks, Nan came to me late one night. She hadn't seen Jimmy for several nights and was driving herself mad with worry and theories. Then she saw you one day a few months later and her fears were confirmed. You were clearly pregnant. It must have been Jimmy's, because we never saw you with anyone else. She tried to speak to you but was scared off. Out of all the things that broke her heart, you and your child were at the top of the list. She didn't live long enough to tell you, so I'm telling you now.

"So you always knew. All those years? Why didn't you tell me all this? Why didn't you tell Julie?"

"It was never a secret for me to tell. When Nan didn't find a chance, I wasn't going to force it out. But now that Jimmy is here and reaching out, I knew I had to speak out. You've always known, but why didn't you tell him?"

Lisa shrugged and put her hands over her face.

Liz touched her shoulder and let herself out.

Matt bumped into Jamie on his way back. They both walked together towards their house. They opened the door to delicious smells of homemade curry, the sound of music and laughter. Simon was dancing round a bubbling pot of curry and Julie was sitting on a kitchen chair laughing at him.

"Boys! You're just in time for my magnificent curry! Julie tells me she's never made one so today's the day!"

Matt and Jamie shared a look. They'd had curry before, but now wasn't the time to tell Simon that. Matt got the cutlery out and Jamie took charge of the drinks. Simon put mats out for the curry, rice and naan.

"Did you make that all yourself?"

Simon gave a bow.

"You're hired!" laughed Jamie.

They all sat round the table and started to eat. Julie looked round at each face and smiled,

"This is the life isn't it?"

Matt glanced up and met her eyes,

"It is."

Jamie pushed his chair back, his cheeks aflame,

"Too hot for you there Jamie?"

Jamie necked a glass of milk and wiped his mouth,

"Just a touch."

They all laughed then. Simon closed his hand over the ring and felt hope rising.

A strange high tea

"How much garlic did you put in that curry Simon? We're all going to land round smelling like an Indian takeaway!"

Simon got close to Julie and sniffed,

"Don't smell anything untoward here."

She giggled and picked up her bag, giving a twirl,

"Is this smart enough for afternoon tea?"

"You're beautiful. As always."

Julie blushed,

"What's got into you?"

Simon shrugged. The boys ambled in, looking a bit better presented than normal. Jamie was still in shorts. Apart from his school uniform, Julie wasn't sure he had a pair of proper trousers to his name. At least they were both in clean clothes and had tidied their hair.

"Am I driving us, or are we walking?"

"Walking of course. It's not far is it Matt?"

Jamie winked and jabbed his brother's ribs, getting a slap on the head in return.

They set off up the hill.

"Hey! Hold up! I'm coming too!"

Julie sucked her breath in as they all turned to see Lisa puff up to them. She had very red lips today and was wearing a denim skirt. Her hair was pulled up into a neat pony tail. Jamie whistled,

"You look great, mum."

"I feel ridiculous. Look at these shoes!"

She pointed down to faded red sandals with straw wedges that she had clearly bought in a thrift shop. Her toe nails were painted red too.

"First pay packet."

Julie nodded,

"Very nice Lisa."

Lisa curtsied and they all headed towards Jimmy's house. Simon squeezed Julie's hand and whispered,

"Well done."

Jimmy was looking out the window for their approach. He flung open the front door,

"Welcome everyone!"

No-one mentioned the faint smell of burning, or the signs of baking panic in the kitchen. Jimmy had dressed up in a pressed shirt and jeans with creases firmly down the middle. He was smelling of cologne, but not enough to cover the baking smells that greeted them all. He ushered them in and gestured to the old once gold living room suite. Lisa was the last to sit down. Jimmy grabbed her hand and led her to the last seat. "Drinks. What can I get you?"

Lisa laughed until Julie cut in,

"Tea would be lovely, thanks. Let me help you."

She followed Jimmy into the kitchen. Liz was there, with a dishcloth in her hand.

"Julie! It's been a while! How are you?"

Liz swayed over to her and gripped a chair to steady herself. She rolled her eyes, "Silly old balance!" Julie smiled back,

"It's great to see you again. I'm doing fine.". She moved over to fill up the kettle.

"I hear you've stolen my best partner in crime, Simon." Liz wagged her finger and laughed. Julie blushed,

"Sorry."

Jimmy looked from one to the other,

"Now tell me, how is it that you two know each other? And what's Simon got to do with it?"

"Sure doesn't Liz have everything to do with everyone round here?! I cleaned the church for her a few years ago. Simon used to work with Liz. Kind of."

"Ah Liz, you really do have a finger in every pie don't you?"

Liz sat down and looked dutifully smug. Julie picked up the cloth and finished wiping down the worktop. She had a handful of flour and searched round for the bin.

"Here, give it to me."

Jimmy flung it into the bin and kicked it behind him.

"Hold on, I've something more."

Julie opened the bin and said nothing when she saw a full batch of badly done scones. He met her eyes and made a face.

"Do you have a mop somewhere? I could clean the floor for you if you like?"

Jimmy shook his head,

"I didn't invite you here to clean. Let's have that cup of tea and taste these scones, which are, I tell you, my first attempt."He winked at Julie and she grinned. Their first shared secret. Julie made the tea and clattered the china cups onto an ancient tea trolley. She put the cream and jam in two separate bowls and set them beside the scones. She lifted one,

"They're still warm. And smell delicious. Good job Jimmy!"

She pushed the rattling trolley across the kitchen linoleum and the worn down carpet in the hall. She glanced in to the living room at her family. Because, she realised, that was what they were. Simon leapt up and helped her navigate the bumps on the carpet. Everyone leant forward as they saw the spread and realised they were hungry.

Simon lifted the two bowls,

"Now, the million dollar question is, which first? Jam, or cream?"

They all laughed and shouted 'jam!'.

Liz came in and shook her head,

"Have any of you tried it the other way?"

"No!"

"Well then, how would you know?"

Matt stood up and lifted a scone,

"Ok, I'll try." He dumped a dollop of cream on first and then hovered with his knife over the jam. "Sorry, I can't do it."

Jamie put a whole scone into his mouth and spoke, showering everyone with crumbs,

"How about neither?!"

Julie shook her head and stood to pour the tea. Simon handed the cups round,

"You two make a good team."

Julie put her head down but Simon smiled at Liz. At least one person agreed with him. He noticed Lisa was still looking tense, glancing between Julie and Jimmy. This was new for her too. Of course it was her mess, but it needed cleaned up now. He wasn't the person to do it though. Much as he wanted to fix everything for Julie. He watched her joking with her brothers, stealing looks at Jimmy. Was there any space for him now?

Julie nudged him,

"Penny for your thoughts?"

He chuckled,

"They're not worth much. Except that I"

"You what?"

Simon coughed and ran his hand over his hair,

"I love you."

"I know that Simon."

Simon pursed his lips and put his head down. Julie did not the say the same back. She was already busy collecting empty plates and cups.

Lisa was watching them with a thoughtful look on her face. Jimmy was looking at her. Liz saw everything. What would all these broken pieces come to?

———

Coming together

Julie lifted her hands out of the suds and dried them,

"I think that's us done now."

Jimmy closed the cupboard door and turned to face her.

"Don't leave it too late, love."

Julie frowned,

"What are you on about?"

Jimmy sighed and raised his hands,

"It's not for me to interfere. You'll get it soon, I hope."

"You're not making any sense. It this to do with Lisa?"

He shook his head and then looked beyond her,

"Simon, you look like you're a man on a mission."

Simon looked at Julie,

"I just need Julie. Can we go outside for a second?"

Julie raised her eyebrows,

"It's not the warmest out there."

"Away out with ye, woman."

Jimmy winked at Simon. Julie followed him outside. He led her to the statue and then dropped to one knee in front of her, holding out the ring.

Julie put her hands over her mouth.

"This has been burning a hole in my pocket for weeks now. Julie, life has not been easy for you, but could you let me in to share it with you? Will you marry me?"

There was a long silence as Simon's face got steadily paler and his smile faded.

Julie looked down at her feet,

"This is too much." She turned away from Simon slowly getting up from his knees, ran past a crestfallen Jimmy, avoided a strangely silent living room and pushed out the front door. She kept her eyes down and hurried down the hill. A voice was calling after her but she kept going, trying not to think, just desperate to get away from all the people pulling at her, expecting too much from her.

"Julie, would you hold up for a second!"

Lisa ran up to her, panting.

"Damn these shoes!"

She stopped for a rest. Julie turned to keep going.

"For dear sake, can we sit down? I'm dying here."

Lisa dropped down on the grass beside the pavement. Julie looked down at her,

"What do you want?"

Lisa sighed,

"I know you'll say I'm too late again, but this time, I'm here and I'm asking, are you ok?"

Julie laughed,

"Oh, I don't know; I found out on Wednesday that my dad is alive and wanting to be in my life now, and today, just then, my boyfriend proposed. It's too much, to up-end my already messed up life. How do I fit it all in? I don't know."

Lisa had taken her wedges off and was rubbing her feet.

"Life's a mess. But for you, it's becoming a good mess. I know a lot of it is my fault and I am so, so" her voice cracked, "so sorry for leaving you. But now, people are coming in who will look after you. And maybe, one day, you will let me too."

Julie sighed and rubbed her face,

"I just need time, Lisa. With everything."

"I know. It's just, well, don't be like me. Take hold of the good before it's too late."

Julie pushed herself up, brushed her skirt and smoothed her hair,

"I know. I'm trying."

She lifted her hand and walked away. Lisa looked after her and stayed put. She followed the clouds scudding across the blue sky and watched her daughter make her way down the hill. She took a couple of deep breaths.

Jimmy stood deliberating for a while, then ducked round the side of his house and headed out the front, drawn to help either his newfound daughter, or the woman he had first made a mother. He knew, deep down, that this story was only just beginning. He saluted the wee boy always watching him. Another lost soul that he had on his list. Some day soon, he would knock on that door. To try and help was better than doing nothing, no matter what the outcome was.

Slapping his feet down the hill, Jimmy laughed to himself; that old statue combined with prayers from the heart was definitely working some wonders today. *Do you see this all mum? I hope so. I'm so sorry you're not here. I'm sorry it took me so long to find my way.*

He spied a disconsolate Lisa sitting on the grass verge and

called out to her,

"You planning on camping out here for the night?"

Jimmy grinned and raised his eyebrows, asking permission to sit beside her.

"How is she?"

"Just a bit overwhelmed. But she'll be ok. I hope."

Jimmy nodded,

"That's good."

Lisa squinted at him,

"Did you follow me? Why?"

A large lorry raced past, making him lean closer and drowning out his words.

"What?"

"I wondered if I could take you out sometime? I know it's all backwards but I'd like to anyway. If you would? Like it I mean?"

Lisa contemplated him for a minute,

"You're a fast-mover! Well, why not? I did like you back then too you know."

She pushed herself up and stepped onto the path barefoot.

Jimmy laughed,

"I remember that about you."

"What?"

"You never cared about what other people thought of you."

Lisa stopped and gave a proud smile,

"Never let them see."

Jimmy stopped beside her and offered his hand,

"But I see you. Don't worry, I won't tell." He squeezed her hand and they smiled at each other.

"She's turned out all right, despite us." Lisa shook her head,

"Don't know how. Who was there for her when I was gone dear knows where? I don't think she had anyone." Lisa stopped again and sighed,

"I don't deserve her. Or Matt or Jamie. Oh Jimmy, what a mess I have made of everything!"

Lisa started to cry and hid her face. Jimmy looked on,

"Do you not think my heart is breaking too? But look what, who, has come out of it all? They are all three pretty spectacular. I see parts of you in all of them. Don't look at me like that, I'm serious."

Jimmy took the sandals and set them down. He grabbed hold of Lisa's hands and looked her straight in the eye.

"We have a chance now to pick up the pieces we've dropped in the past. To be mother and father. Too late to change nappies, teach them how to walk, talk or eat. But never too late to love them."

Lisa cried again and this time Jimmy put his arms around her. They both stayed like that and didn't move until the light changed.

Coming down the hill, Matt and Jamie saw them. They crossed the street. They both knew this was a moment that should not be interrupted.

Liz and Simon

Liz had been in the kitchen when Julie ran away from Simon's proposal. She moved over and pulled out a kitchen chair to sit on.   Poor Julie - years of doing everything by herself. It wasn't surprising that she couldn't believe Simon's proposal. He opened the back door and gave Liz a close-lipped smile. He looked at the way out and sighed. He pulled another chair and sat there with his arms by his sides. The fast-moving clouds were intermittently covering the sun, casting light and shade over the kitchen table. Jimmy opened the back door and thought better of it. Liz pushed herself up and moved to put the kettle on. Simon put his hands up to his face and left them there. Liz made tea and set two mugs on the table. Simon pulled his over and took a sip, staring into space.

"You know she just needs a bit more time."

Simon looked up at the ceiling,

"I have been so careful not to push her before she's ready, but it's hard Liz."

Liz picked up on of Simon's hands and held it,

"We both know that Julie is a damaged bird who needs gentle handling."

She dared to say it,

"Have you talked to God about it?"

Simon laughed,

"What would He care?"

"More than you know."

Simon took away his hand and put them both through his hair,

"I have thought about this, more than before, but I'm just not sure what to say."

Liz smiled,

"Just talk to Him the way you would talk to me. From your heart."

"My heart's just been broken Liz."

Liz shook her head,

"This is only a shaky start, not the end. Simon, you are stepping into the broken shell of a dysfunctional family, as husband and father. Tread softly."

Simon's eyes filled.

"It's just so hard. Why couldn't I just meet a girl with no baggage?"

"But you didn't. You met Julie. And Matt and Jamie. And you love them all."

"God, I do."

"Then don't tell me. Tell Him."

Liz stood up, put her hand on his shoulder and left the room, closing the door gently behind her.

After a few minutes of sitting up and slumping down again Simon put this hands together, bent his head and started to pray.

Again, St Anthony saw.

The final piece

Christine knew it was a pointless thing to do, but she couldn't seem to switch her heart off. A running dog, paw prints, the statue and most of all, Tony, were frequent features in her dreams. She knew, whatever the knots around this one, it was a story that deserved to be lived. And so she made her way back to St Anthony. Again. Her blond ponytail swung with every step. Her high heels hit the pavement in time with her pounding heart. There was an elderly man in one of the gardens who reminded her of Mr Connelly, her rose pruning knight from darker days. She smiled at him and he lifted his trowel to her. It was a peaceful, friendly street, the total opposite to the mansion-lined road where she used to live. She shut her eyes to the memory of that time. Mum told her she should go talk to someone trained in these things, but Christine was too frightened of facing those dragons she found were best kept pushed down. Life had raced on for her sister Geraldine, but it felt frozen for Christine. Her mum asked her almost every day what her plans were, and she always made something up but the fact was, her future was blank. Lonely.

Just as Christine neared the house, a flash of brown tore

past her. She kept going, saw that the car was away today, but still lifted the latch on the gate and followed the path towards the statue and the dog digging in a frenzy beneath it. Her heart was thumping but she didn't look behind her. She sat down on the seat and put her shaking hands together. When she heard the latch click open, she stood up. And he was there, standing in front of her, the man who had been her hope, her protector, her promise of better people, better things, a better life.

They both looked at each other and began to smile. It had been years since he had lain in front of the church door to stop Gavin from reaching her. The days of snatched conversations and stolen flowers were long gone. She wondered if he knew that she had left Gavin. How would he? For some reason, it felt important that he knew. Tony just stood there, kept back by all the questions on his mind. He looked at Christine again and laughed quietly,

"Well this is strange. I mean, you being here. And St Anthony. And me."

Christine nodded,

"It is an odd place for him to be, that's for sure. I wonder…"

Tony told her about Jimmy's compulsion to save the statue. Christine had heard it all before, but she didn't stop him. She looked at his neat haircut, his ironed shirt, his clean hands. He finished speaking and caught her examining him.

"A bit different I know," he flushed.

Christine nodded,

"You look well, Tony."

"Would you have recognised me if it wasn't for Faithful?"

It was Christine's turn to blush. She tucked her loose strands behind her ear and re-buttoned her cardigan.

"I would never forget your eyes."

Tony swallowed and took a step forward.

"I'm glad. There are things I should…"

"Me too."

Christine sat down again, and made space for him to sit next to her. He stayed standing,

"I actually need to get back to work so…"

Christine gave a disappointed cough.

"Tony, in case this is my only chance, I wanted you to know that you always have my heart. You are my heart. Whatever the complications."

Tony took in her shaking hands and flushed face. This wasn't something to walk away from. He shut his eyes to all the objections flooding his mind,

"I'm sorry Christine, I can't."

And then he started to walk away.

Christine ran after him,

"Wait! I know you are his brother. I guessed a while ago but it doesn't change how I feel. You are light, he is shade. It's been years and I don't see why he should win over my choices now. He can't."

Tony's eyes filled.

"But it might wreck everything."

"So we won't let it."

Christine stretched her slim hand out. Tony sighed and reached out his strong one to take it. They stood like that until Faithful started to pull on the lead.

"Can I walk you to work? I can take Faithful back with me if you like?"

Tony smiled and shook his head,

"What's happened to the timid, scared girl I once knew?"

"She broke free, and listened to her heart."

Tony got closer, lifted his arms around her and kissed her hair.

"You are more than I deserve. Much, much more."

Christine stepped back, shook her head and smiled.

The last piece had fallen into its rightful place.

A fresh start

It was the longest day of summer. The strong sun was making everything appear dusty and hot. Even St Anthony looked like he was melting. Liz and Jamie were in fits of giggles, draping garlands of flowers over the once imposing statue.

"Is this blasphemous Liz?"

Liz looked at the wreath Jamie was adjusting on top of St Anthony's head and gave a nod of approval,

"Using nature's beauty to adorn a lifeless statue is far from blasphemy Jamie. I personally think it's the opposite."

"It's not like we're drawing rude pictures on him I suppose. I meant to ask you, where is my favourite sculpture now?"

Liz smiled,

"Why? You thinking about stealing it again?"

Jamie made a face,

"Duh, of course not."

"I have it in my living room. It's my favourite too."

Liz shielded her eyes and looked up at Jamie,

"How are you doing after your dad signed off with you? Matt told me."

Jamie climbed down the ladder, straightened his tie and smoothed down his curly hair,

"I had moved on from him a long time ago. Sure we've got Simon now."

"You do. There's a man who'll always do his best for you."

Liz unhooked another garland from the bunch on her arm and put it on her recently set hair,

"How do I look?"

Jamie put his index finger to his mouth and appraised her,

"Pretty well, but I think you need to lose the slippers."

Liz looked down at her feet and gasped,

"I totally forgot I still had those on! That would make a statement wouldn't it?!"

Jamie was off looking for a spade so her words were lost. She squinted up at the statue,

"You wouldn't care would you? I'm certain the bride and groom won't either."

Father of all these children, I pray You would bless and keep each one. They were never lost to You.

Liz opened her eyes and smiled, thinking about the reunion of Christine and Tony, the family that was Julie, Simon, Matt and Jamie and now the coming together of the two most lost, most broken ones of all. Today, she was bringing them together. Her purpose had become clear again.

Jimmy peered out at the garden from his bedroom window and marvelled at the difference a few months had made. He'd done one spontaneous thing back then, and look how many people had been helped. His mother smiled at him from her sepia-tinted photo. He checked his tie and looked round,

"Are you ready Matt?"

Matt stepped forward and Jimmy clapped his hands,

"Let's go get me married."